D1495306

A PARCEL OF LIFE

Lucinda Roberts

A Parcel of Life
© Lucinda Roberts 2016

Cover: Linocut by Celia Lewis ~ *www.celialewis.co.uk*

All rights reserved. The moral right of the author has been asserted.

Also by the author:
Middle Age Spread

~ Luck of the Draw Publications ~

LUCINDA ROBERTS

CONTENTS

A PARCEL OF LIFE

BOOK ONE: AFTER THE SWALLOWS

He had rented the bungalow for six months, the time they said it would take the damaged nerves in his spine to heal. There was a possibility that the regeneration process might take longer, the suave, cold-eyed consultant had said. An option to renew the tenancy after the first six months was available, but half a year away did not concern him at the moment.

The bungalow was a plain dwelling but the wheelchair fitted perfectly and it was, as advertised, designed and equipped for an invalid. He could not think of himself as such but that in fact was what he had become. The skiing accident had left him partially paralysed, and although they constantly told him how lucky he was to be alive, there were many times when he was not so sure he agreed with them.

He had grown weary of having pins stuck in the soles of his feet, sick of painful operations, of not being allowed to smoke, drink or move. Of not even being allowed to get randy when the crisp blond nurse with a provocative arse gave him a bed bath.

Now at least that was all over and he was on his own to make what he liked of the healing process. Don't push it, the physiotherapist had advised, just work your way back gradually and let the pain be your guide. Well, there was plenty of that, and the blessed injections that had sent him off to another planet had long since ceased. The painkillers he'd been prescribed were a help, but he tried to take them as little as possible. Pills had never been on his menu.

The nights were hell, and when morning came the face that stared back at him in the mirror was sallow and lined, a bitter reminder of what he had become. He resolved to grow a beard to avoid the detailed inspection of his face necessitated by the morning shave.

The local health authority had provided him with a daily carer whose name was Bates. She had been there to greet him, but she was a brisk, plain woman with no knowledge of compassion or laughter, and he knew instinctively that she would be no help to his recovery in spite of her efficient manner and medical competence.

Clearly she was not a long-term prospect, but he would bide his time and endure being treated like a baby until he felt in a position to make other arrangements. What these might be exactly he had yet to work out. All that he required to be done for him could be done by a good woman who could cook and clean and keep her own counsel. What this as yet unknown person might say to her friends in the village was of no concern to him at all, as long as she kept her gossip and chatter away from the bungalow.

The bungalow was called Moor View. This was not surprising, as views of the moor were exactly what it had. Although he had been born and raised in the country and had enjoyed his rural environment as a child, he had never, in adult life, bothered much about his surroundings. What he had been doing had always seemed more important than where he was.

Both his parents were dead, and taxes and outmoded ideas had long ago necessitated the sale of the old family home, thus severing any remaining links he had had with his roots. He was the last of his line apart from an elder sister who had married an Australian sheep farmer and gone to live in the outback.

Christmas cards arrived each year, enclosing photographs of a growing brood of strong, sun tanned children who meant nothing to him at all. He experienced a fleeting sadness once a year that this was the case, but Daphne was 10 years older than he was and they had never been close. Her children and their way of life were alien and his nieces and nephews were unlikely to have any use for an unknown and crippled uncle in a far off land.

Perhaps one day if they ever came over to England, he would try to take an interest in them, but secretly he hoped that this would never happen. They would probably be uncouth and brash and speak about things he would not understand, or only bother with him because they hoped to inherit his money.

For now his life would revolve around recovery and Moor View seemed the ideal place. The owner's late husband had been in a wheelchair so the bungalow was well adapted for that purpose. On his death she had decided to go and live with her daughter and rent it out. It was aptly named, as the large sitting room window gave wonderful views out over the moor which was beginning to come to life after the long winter.

The fresh green of the sprouting bracken and the golden yellow gorse flowers had broken through the dead growth of last year and the flat, white grass was beginning to move again. The banks in the lane were full of primroses, campion and stitchwort and red deer could sometimes be seen, wandering slowly up the combe. Buzzards, too, were regular inhabitants, their eerie mewing as they soared and circled a sharp contrast to the harsh *kaaah* of the crows.

Some previous occupant must have been a keen bird watcher for outside the window was a large bird table hung with empty feeders. The passage of time had done its work and rust had attacked the feeders, leaving them with an air of sad neglect and abandonment.

From the big window he could see the back of a long, low range of stone buildings, bounded by an untidy wall from which sprouted tufts of fern and grass. Between the wall and the buildings was a small area of fenced rough grass, a vegetable garden and a large greenhouse. So somebody else lived up here after all, he thought. He hoped whoever it was would not prove to be nosey or do-gooding neighbours, intent on *popping-in* to cheer him up. He would have to tell Bates that he had no wish to receive visitors.

His train of thought led him on to Bates herself. He must telephone the agency and tell them that she did not suit him and that he wished her to be gone. He would try this afternoon when she went to the village to buy stores and, he suspected, tell everyone what a miserable, unfriendly creature her latest charge had turned out to be.

A movement in the bungalow garden caught his eye and he saw a bent old man carrying some tools move slowly across the small square of lawn to the flowerbed.

The man glanced up and, seeing he was being watched, frowned, turned away and plodded on towards his tasks. *A man after my own heart* he thought as his mouth twisted into the ghost of a smile.

'Who's the gardener?' he called out to Bates.

'That's old Mr Rawle. He lives in the village – he's been looking after this garden for years. He's a sour old man, dirty too, but he never comes into the house. Good at his job though I suppose.'

Perhaps Mr Rawle would provide the answer to his problem. If he had been around for so long, he must surely know everybody who lived in the village, and be able to suggest someone who might like the job of keeping house for him. The spring sun was warm and soporific through the glass and he dozed off.

The sound of the front door shutting woke him up and proclaimed the departure of Bates to the village where she usually stayed for an hour or so while he was resting. He saw Rawle sitting outside the shed enjoying his tea and tobacco in the sun, and wheeled himself down the concrete path to where the old man was relaxing.

The old man glanced up at the sound of the wheelchair and touched his cap briefly with a grimy finger, the gesture indicating respect but not friendship.

He decided that the direct approach would serve him best and that platitudes about the beauty of the day and the state of the garden would not impress the old man.

'Afternoon Mr. Rawle.'

'Zurr.'

'I need someone to help in the house and thought you might know of somebody.'

'What's with 'ers then?' Rawle nodded towards the house.

'I don't need her fussing over me – I just need someone quiet for 2 or 3 hours housekeeping a day – cooking, shopping, cleaning – that sort of thing.'

'Hmm – know what you mean.'

Rawle slowly put down his chipped enamel mug and stared in silent thought. He spat, and the spittle shot expertly out through a gap in his brown teeth, landing on the path by the wheelchair.

'M'sister Martha Westcott – she'd do. Widow, boys gone city ways, don't yap much.'

'Could you ask her for me? I'd be very grateful.'

'Leave't with me.' He picked up the mug and slowly stood up, clearly indicating that the matter was closed.

If Mrs Westcott was anything like her brother she would do well, although he hoped perhaps she might be cleaner and less inclined to spit. He wheeled himself back into the house to telephone the agency before Bates returned. He knew he would have to tell her himself of the anticipated new arrangement and decided to do that this evening to avoid any embarrassment if Mrs Westcott were to arrive in the morning.

He went back to his spot by the window feeling absurdly pleased with himself. He had made a decision of his own after a year of having others decide his life for him, and it was as if a tiny drop of new blood had seeped into his veins. He would have enjoyed a drink but that would have to wait until tomorrow when Mrs Westcott's instructions would include whisky on the shopping list, hitherto banned by Bates.

For no particular reason, his unfocused eyes were resting on the stone buildings when the door opened and a woman came out closely followed by a fawn coloured lurcher dog. So this was his neighbour! His instinctive reaction was to push back out of sight but he realised that from that distance she could not possibly see that he was watching her. She was wearing loose fitting red trousers and a floppy hat, which largely obscured her face. It was impossible to tell her age, but her movements had neither the supple haste of youth nor the slow care of old age.

The woman was carrying a bucket, which she took over to the low fence that separated the garden from the rough grass and tipped the contents onto the ground. Immediately a small pink pig ran up and started eating greedily, stopping only briefly to acknowledge the affectionate rubs she was giving it.

The dog had obviously seen it all before, and looked bored and superior as it lay down by the barn wall. Having finished with the pig, the woman went into the greenhouse where she moved steadily through the late afternoon ritual of tending the plants and shutting the house up, for the nights were still cold up on the moor.

Her actions were economic and unhurried and seemed to create an aura of great concentration and pleasure in what she was doing. He turned away, feeling almost as if he were intruding, but he was somehow reassured that this person and her dog would offer no threat to his privacy.

Bates returned, and with her all the tension that the quiet afternoon had begun to dispel. He braced himself for the inevitable disapproval that would follow his announcement of the possible arrival of Mrs Westcott, and her own departure.

Once, he would not have given a second thought to an interview of this nature. Once, he had been a different person. Life had not always been like this but then, of course, there had been Isobel.

*

It had been love at first sight. As she streaked past the post to win the sisters' race at his prep school, he had never seen anything more beautiful. Her long brown legs had skimmed over the parched turf of the school playing fields, her dishevelled auburn hair bouncing on her shoulders as she smiled her victory smile.

He turned to the boy standing beside him to ask casually the identity of the winning girl. The boy was called Peter Frampton, and they were of similar age, but were acquaintances rather than good friends. With little interest Peter replied that she was his sister, younger by two years, pretty annoying at times but not bad for a girl. Frampton wandered off to find his parents and he was left alone with the realisation that his passport to happiness lay in friendship with this boy. Only through him could he hope to meet and get to know this heavenly creature.

He discovered that Peter lived in Sussex where his father farmed. His own home was in Cheshire so there was obviously no possibility of a chance meeting, or of a friendship developing between the two families.

A feeling of fellowship had grown between the two boys during the winter term when they discovered they had much in common and he felt the time had arrived when he could invite Peter Frampton to stay with him during the Christmas holidays. Perhaps Peter would then return his hospitality and he would at last have a chance to meet his friend's beautiful sister, who he learnt was called Isobel.

Peter's visit was a success and the boys vowed to see more of each other when they returned to school after

Christmas. Their affinity strengthened and the only cause of mild discord between them was his obsession with Isobel. It made Peter laugh and although he agreed that she was alright as sisters go, he could not see that there was anything particularly special about her.

The invitation to stay with the Framptons arrived at the beginning of the long summer holidays and was eagerly accepted, although his mother was a little disappointed at his apparent longing to leave his own family and home.

He could not possibly tell her the reason why, as she was an introverted, distant woman and their relationship did not extend to confidences. She was perfectly able to accept that her son was growing up, and that his own life would soon take over from the life which she had considered it her duty to impose on him.

She put him on the train and Peter and his mother met him at their local railway station. Isobel, he learned, was at Pony Club camp and they were all to go over the next day to watch her compete in the end of camp gymkhana. The thought filled him with joy and terror all at the same time and, as they approached the farm where the camp was held, he experienced a gripping nervousness that he had never felt before.

Isobel dashed up to greet her family. She was immaculately dressed and rode her pony as if born on it. Her pockets were stuffed with rosettes which she handed to her mother who told Peter to introduce his friend. He felt his face flush red as she smiled and said hello before riding off to the next event.

He was to wait nearly ten years before he saw her again, but the image of her loveliness never left his mind. He and Peter had gone on to different schools and different lives and inevitably their friendship had dwindled and died as they lost contact.

It was at a party in London that he saw her again and the recognition was instant. She was with her brother and a man called Felix Miller who was at university with Peter. It was a reunion which delighted them all, and Felix suggested that they should celebrate by dining out together after the drinks party.

The next six months passed in a haze of happiness, for Isobel was his. They delighted in each other's company and at night, her slender body gave him a joy and fulfilment he had never known could exist. His whole universe revolved around her and everything he did or saw was filled with new enthusiasm and charm. He knew that without her, his life would be empty. That was before the telephone call.

Her voice sounded strangled and thick as she told him that Peter was dead – killed in a freak accident with a tractor. She begged him to come down to Sussex immediately to help support her and her distraught parents.

He had been deeply shocked, not only by the death of his friend, but also by the shameful feeling of pleasure he was unable to suppress that it had been him that she had turned to in her grief. He had gone down to Sussex immediately and to his best ability had helped them through the nightmare of Peter's funeral and the disposal of his unwanted possessions. Peter's parents were grateful and assured him they would look forward to his next visit, but Isobel seemed unable to come to terms with her brother's death.

Without Peter she appeared to change and although they continued to see each other, he sensed a withdrawal in her and a hardening of her personality. Also he suspected that she was seeing other men.

They had gone down to the country to stay for a few days with Isobel's parents but the old sunny atmosphere had gone. The Framptons were brave in their struggle to accept their only son's death, but their lost sparkle had somehow taken with it their physical stature and they had become old and tired. The house no longer seemed the bright, noisy haven it had once been and a listless air of dejection permeated the rooms. After dinner on their last night, Isobel had taken him out into the yard, where they sat together, watching the swallows swooping and diving, grabbing the last moments of daylight before going to roost in the old barns.

Dinner had been early that night but dusk had fallen, for autumn was round the corner and the trees were turning. She had told him then of the sadness she felt when the swallows had gone. How their lining up on the wires prior to their migration had always depressed her, but their return in the spring filled her with new hope and joy. Could it be like that again next spring she had wondered, with her brother gone.

It was then that he asked her to marry him; when his whole world hung on her answer. She had turned away and walked slowly to an old stone mounting block where she sat fiddling with the weeds growing out of a crack in the surface. She told him that she loved him but had begged for time as she was still very upset by Peter's death. He longed to tell her that his devotion would only ease her pain, but he could find no words to express the intensity of his passion.

It was only a few weeks after their encounter in the stable yard that he read in the paper of her engagement to Felix Miller. He had gone out, got very drunk, and ended up in bed with a prostitute. But in the morning he had just felt ill and sordid. He received a sad and apologetic letter from Isobel's mother, who alone had understood the depth of his feeling for her daughter. Her letter tried to explain how Isobel's love for her brother had caused her to give herself to Felix and how, because he had been Peter's special friend, she could somehow recreate their sibling bond through marriage to him.

He was grateful for Mrs Frampton's kindness and

insight but his reply was false in its fortitude. He had no wish to add to her sorrow by telling her that her daughter's action had devastated his whole existence. He had gone away soon afterwards, to the farthest ends of the earth, and he had never communicated with the Frampton family again. The swallows had flown and so had Isobel.

*

Martha Westcott arrived as promised the following morning. His interview with Nurse Bates had been short and uneasy, but in the end they had shaken hands and parted on reasonable terms. She had shrugged her shoulders and wished him well before moving on to find a new patient who he hoped would appreciate her endeavours more than he had.

Martha Westcott was everything he had hoped she might be, and he liked her immediately. She was a tall gaunt woman in her early 60s who must once have been striking, for her features were fine but strong and she bore little resemblance to her brother. Her manner was direct but polite and she had a quiet dignity about her that he recognised and respected. Here was a woman whose presence would not trouble him and whose care he would value.

He held out his hand and smiled and, after a fractional hesitation, she took it and smiled back. He slept better that night than he had for a very long time and when the early sun fell on his face he did not resent the coming of the day. Perhaps he would try harder with his exercises and spend more time in the garden while the weather was good. Today was not one of the old man's working days so he would be alone and unwatched when he attempted the few steps they had advised him to start with.

It was hard, depressing work and as the sky clouded over and rain threatened, he moved back indoors. He was beginning to find himself drawn to the big window where he would sit for hours, gazing out over the moor. It was a restful and undemanding pastime and although he would often try and read, he usually fell asleep with the book open on his lap.

The woman with the dog had not appeared again since his first sighting. He was surprised about this, as he knew it was a busy time of year in the vegetable garden and she had seemed dedicated to her growing. Perhaps she had gone away somewhere for a few days and taken the dog with her, leaving someone to feed the pig. Her whereabouts was of no particular interest and there was always the fear, too, that his initial assessment might be wrong and she would turn out to be inquisitive after all.

This particular afternoon though, almost as if in response to his thoughts, she appeared. He had just woken up when he saw her come out of the buildings. The rain, no more than a shower, had passed and the sun that followed gave promise of a lovely fresh evening. She was wearing exactly the same clothes as before, the red trousers, the floppy hat and the dog was there too. She worked steadily, stopping occasionally to ease her back and speak to the dog, who responded with a slight movement of its tail. The pig seemed uninterested, and having stood and watched for a while with its snout pressed through the wire, turned away to resume the more gainful activity of rooting up its enclosure.

The plot was still bare, for this was high ground and the soil stayed cold until well on into the spring, but her trug was full of seed packets and row markers and sowing was clearly the task for the day.

The dog seemed to know instinctively when its owner was about to finish work, for it suddenly stood up and, after yawning and stretching its long thin body, went and stood by the barn door with its ears cocked expectantly. She tidied the debris of seed packets and, having collected up her tools, stood for a moment to admire her work before being preceded by the dog back through the door and out of sight.

The swallows continued to swoop in and out through the doorway, working hard towards the rearing of their broods and the long flight south that they would undertake in the autumn.

He turned the wheelchair and propelled himself to the kitchen to pour his evening whisky. Soon he hoped to be walking the few steps necessary to fulfil this task, but he did not yet feel courageous enough to risk failure. The wheelchair had grown to represent security, not only physical but mental too. At first he had hated it and had felt reduced by his dependence upon it, but then gradually he had sunk back into the comfort it had to offer. To him, cripples were allowed to be morose and reclusive, for life had dealt them a rotten hand. Normal healthy people could overlook bad manners with an indulgence that came from the relief that it was not themselves who were the victims of misfortune. He never perceived his own miserable attitude as self-pity, merely another part of a life full of affliction and futility.

He slept well again that night, and the dreams and pain that had tormented him for so long began to diminish and leave him in peace. As spring moved quietly into summer, he felt an unaccustomed spark of interest flicker inside him.

The moor changed her clothing, and great spears of purple foxgloves pushed up through the nettles and ferns that grew out of the banks and hedgerows. The woman's vegetables were growing well, and now he could see the rows of plants showing green through the soil. The pig grew too. Hour after hour the woman in the red trousers worked on the plot; thinning, planting out, feeding and hoeing. The routine never changed, always the same time, the same clothes and the dog, which lay in the same place. He found this reassuring and came to look forward to their silent and unacknowledged companionship.

Much to his surprise, he even became interested in the progress of the vegetables and began to look forward to the afternoon, when he would take up his position by the big window and study their growth whilst awaiting the arrival of their tender.

His initial liking of Martha Westcott had not lessened, and in their own strange ways they had become friends. Few words passed between them but their relationship had no need for unnecessary chatter and she never questioned his requests or complained about his moods. The black moments still came and with them the vision of Isobel which he had tried so hard to eradicate. But these moments were becoming less frequent and the fight against them easier to win.

His physical condition was improving as well, and he no longer dreaded the effort he knew he would have to make to achieve the modest targets he set himself. A determination to succeed had replaced the indifference he had felt during the first few weeks at Moor View and he was now able, with the help of two sticks, to walk slowly round the small garden several times a day.

The fine weather that had lasted well on into summer broke suddenly and rain swept in from the Atlantic, shrouding the moor and blotting out the view. He felt oppressed by this blanket of mist and drizzle and he hated it. At first he tried to continue his walking exercises in the house, but it was unsatisfactory and after two days he gave it up. He felt restless and dispirited and he realised that the cause of this was the reduced likelihood of seeing the woman in the garden. He had not understood how important this interlude in his day had become, nor could he comprehend why this should be. The unknown woman intrigued him and he found he missed watching her and the dog.

The rain continued and with it his depression. He still went and sat by the window as it had become a habit that he saw no reason to break. On the fourth day he was rewarded when, in spite of the continuing rain, she came through the door, carrying a large basket.

The dog did not come out of the barn but stood waiting in the doorway, watching. Clearly she had come only to harvest some produce and to check the greenhouse, and had made no concession to the rain by wearing a mackintosh. She bent and picked for some while and, having filled the basket, straightened up and paused for a moment to stretch. The rain had soaked her shirt and as she pulled back her shoulders, it clung to her body, showing clearly the outline of her breasts. She picked up the now full basket and was gone, led back through the door by the dog.

He stared after her, for the experience had both excited and disturbed him. Sex had not been a factor in his life for so long that his celibate state had ceased to concern him. Now suddenly, this visual encounter had rekindled a suppressed desire that he could not satisfy. He turned away from the window, angry that this had happened and determined to put it out of his mind. He would give up his daily vigil and change his routine, thus blotting her out of his thoughts. It was ridiculous to feel this way about someone he had never met and knew nothing about.

The rain stopped and was replaced once more with sunshine. He fought and won the battle to stay away from the window for five days but on the sixth, like a magnet, it drew him back.

The warm, damp weather had accelerated the growth of the vegetables and the plot was now a green sea of vegetation, splashed with the red of runner bean flowers and tomatoes. Summer was drifting on and the swallows were already beginning to teach their young to fly, the adults in close attendance to demonstrate their graceful art to the hesitant fledglings.

She was there again, as he knew she would be, and his

heart turned over and was full of happiness. All his anger and confusion left him, and he knew that this simple phenomenon had brought hope back into his life.

He was tempted to ask Martha Westcott who the woman was for he was certain that she would know all about her, but something stopped him. Perhaps when the lease expired and he was preparing to leave, he would find out. She was most probably a happily married housewife and leading member of the local Women's Institute. In the meantime he would continue to work at his rehabilitation and postpone for the moment any thoughts concerning his future.

A sultry, changeable August gave way to September. The grasses and ferns began to look tired, and even the moorland creatures seemed to lose their summer insouciance. The season was dying and soon winter would spread her tentacles over the land. At first he feared to see the swallows lining up on the wires, for they were a stark reminder of Isobel and his long buried past. It was with relief that he realised that these thoughts no longer brought the old familiar pain and he was able to think about what had been with some equanimity.

The woman continued to visit the garden but these visits were now brief, being largely limited to picking the remaining vegetables and clearing the redundant debris of the dying plants. The daylight hours were diminishing and the trees beginning to take on their autumn hue.

He was now able to walk for short distances with only one stick and had, some time ago, thrown away all the pills he had been prescribed. The wheelchair was gathering dust in the spare bedroom and, no longer afraid of his own face, he had shaved off the scruffy beard he had tried to grow when he first arrived. He knew that Martha Westcott delighted in his progress and he noticed without comment, that she had gradually increased the size of the meals she left ready for him. Her brother continued to tend the small garden but only came once a week for there was little work to be done now. He was glad of this, as he had never liked the old man and his presence had inhibited the time he liked to spend outdoors.

He noticed one day that the pig was no longer in its pen, and supposed that it must have gone for slaughter as it had grown large during the summer. He felt sorry about this for it had seemed an amiable, friendly creature, but then death would always come for every living thing in the end and the pig's life, albeit short, had certainly been good. Better the lot of the pig perhaps than that of many human beings.

One day the woman came early to the plot. It was only by chance that he saw her and he wondered what this change of routine might mean. Everything else was the same, the red trousers, the old hat and the dog, but her movements were somehow different.

The easy relaxed attitude that had given an aura of pleasure and devotion to her labours was replaced by a feeling of anxious urgency. Even the dog seemed unsettled and forsook its customary spot, wandering around and never taking its eyes off its owner. She finished tidying up and strode immediately back through the door, pulling it shut with an air of finality.

She did not come again, as he knew she would not. It was time for him to go too, for he could not contemplate living at Moor View through the winter without her proximity.

He would ask Martha Westcott about her now that it was nearly all over.

'I've been watching that woman with the dog over there working in her vegetable garden – do you know who she is?'

'Why yes – she's called Miss Barstow. A very nice lady by all accounts – private sort of a person – bin here ooh…

bout 11 year or so.'

'Has she got family that you know of?'

'No, just her I think. Don't know much about her to tell you the truth but she's well liked down the village. She'll be gone soon.'

'Oh no, I feared as much,' he couldn't stop himself.

'Don't you worry, she's like them swallows – off and away for the winter to some furrin place. When they come back, so will she.'

'Shall I come back too do you think?'

'Course you shall,' Martha nodded as if it was a foregone conclusion.

'Do you know her Christian name by any chance?'

'Why yes,' she said after a moment's thought. 'It's Isobel.'

They smiled at one another in understanding.

BOOK TWO: THE FANTASY

Iona Jane Cridland arrived without fuss or bother on her mother's thirty-seventh birthday. Mrs Cridland called her *my little gift from God*, though most people assumed that Arthur Cridland had been the deity responsible for Iona's creation.

Iona Jane was the result of the only daring act that her parents had ever undertaken in their normally drab and careful lives, and from this had sprung not only herself but also her name.

It seemed unlikely that the heritage and gift of children was to be bestowed upon the Cridlands when, after 10 years of marriage, they decided to celebrate Arthur's promotion to under manager at his local bank, by hitching up their small caravan and departing for the unknown territory of the west coast of Scotland.

As the rain pattered down and the midges bit, they took the ferry bound for the Isle of Mull. There they parked the caravan and planned their itinerary for the few days they would spend on the island. Every tourist information leaflet which they had carefully studied suggested that a visit to the isle of Iona was not to be missed. So they donned their plastic mackintoshes, filled a flask with tea and crossed the Sound to the hallowed Isle.

The ancient Celtic ruins stirred a lust in Arthur's loins, unknown and untapped since their honeymoon in a Brighton guest house, and when they returned to Mull, the caravan rocked briefly and Iona Jane began her passage through life.

When Mrs Cridland realised that the changes which were occurring in her body could only mean one thing, she rushed first to her doctor for confirmation, and second to her local church to give thanks to the good Lord for what she could only perceive as a miracle.

Her triumphant announcement to Arthur was received with a grunt through the stem of his pipe and a tentative peck on the cheek. Mrs Cridland was convinced from the start that her child would be a girl, and thus the small spare bedroom was decorated from floor to ceiling in pink. Frills, friezes, flounces and bunny rabbits created a giant womb, and all that remained to be settled was the infant's name.

With his liking for familiarity, Arthur favoured Jane, but the expectant mother was emphatic. The child must be named Iona. After all, was it not the ancient mystique of the island that had provided the catalyst for this miraculous event. He wondered what would happen if the child should turn out to be a boy but wisely kept his thoughts to himself. Iona Jane never let anybody down, she was just not that sort of person, and she started life as she meant to go on. She arrived on time, trouble-free, crumpled and slimy but female.

The caravan never rocked again, and Iona was reared with the care and devotion often lavished on the only child of older parents. Life at 28 Parkend Road in respectable suburbia was secure, peaceful and dull.

Every day Iona came home from school and had her tea, and after tea she settled down to do her homework. When this was finished her time was her own, although she was seldom left to enjoy it as she wished. Television was not encouraged and her mother, believing that idle fingers made idle minds, joined her daughter in an endless orgy of handicrafts and board games, which provided occupation until her father returned from the bank. When he had settled with his pipe and slippers, Iona was obliged to repeat to him the events of her day, which she had already recounted to her mother during tea.

Iona was an entirely middling sort of a child, neither thin nor fat, pretty nor ugly, bright nor dim. She joined in everything to a modest degree and was well enough liked by her peers without commanding the popularity and worship which small girls can bestow on their more charismatic peers.

When she was 11 years old, *Alice in Wonderland* was chosen as the Christmas play to be performed at the end of term. The play was an important feature of school life, and the excited anticipation that surrounded the casting for the production was as great as in any professional theatre company.

The aspiring thespians gathered anxiously to hear the outcome of the auditions, and Iona assumed that she would be cast as some insignificant tree or insect. Her astonishment was as great as everyone else's when she learned that she had been chosen to play the title role. One or two of the more spiteful girls, who were disappointed at not being picked themselves, put the choice down to Iona's hair which, when not confined in two tight pigtails, fell down her back in a chestnut cascade. Her overjoyed mother started immediately to make the most beautiful Alice costume ever created and life at Parkend Road began to resemble a fall down the rabbit hole into wonderland.

Her daughter was to be the most perfect Alice ever seen and indeed she was. Mrs Cridland nearly burst with pride as her little miracle performed without fault and the rafters of the local village hall rang to the applause of the assembled audience.

Iona herself could not understand what all the fuss was about for to her, acting was the easiest thing in the world. She had spent most of her eleven years acting as she was seldom Iona Cridland, an ordinary girl from suburbia, but a beautiful imaginary girl whose life was one great romantic adventure.

Knights in shining armour galloped through her dreams; handsome white-coated doctors fell in love with her as they carried out life-saving operations; indeed all manner of wonderful male creatures fired her imagination. She would weave extraordinary stories and adventures around her fantasy men, herself the heroine, they in turn the all-conquering heroes who would carry her away to a life of eternal bliss.

What happened beyond that was as yet unclear, for Iona was only on the brink of sexual realisation and had no more than a vague idea that *something* took place between men and women that resulted in babies. Sex was not discussed at 28 Parkend Road.

As Iona approached her twelfth birthday her mother, fearing the influence of her school friends, took her daughter aside and with some agitation tried to explain the facts of life. After some rather vague references to eggs and tadpoles, she thrust a small booklet into Iona's hand and retired satisfied that her maternal duty was done.

Unbeknown to her mother, Iona knew all about eggs and tadpoles and a lot more besides. Her little school friends, as her mother feared, had long since acquainted her with *what went on*. Many had older brothers and sisters to help with their education, and the information gathered was eagerly shared amongst class-mates, often greatly exaggerated and embellished with lurid diagrams.

Iona thought deeply about the whole subject, and decided that her virginity was beyond price and should be carefully guarded for the moment when the man of her fantasy would materialise as a flesh and blood human being. She never doubted that this would happen, and as the years passed and she listened to her friends' descriptions of their deflowering, she became even more convinced that she was doing the right thing.

They sniggered and giggled and proudly pointed out foul spotty youths who had clambered aboard and popped their willing hymens with about as much sensitivity as an animal. Their descriptions of the grunts and smells that accompanied the act bore no resemblance to Iona's vision of this mystical and significant event.

In her last year at school Iona was far too busy studying for her A Levels to spend much time on anything else. She was not naturally brilliant and her scholastic achievements were entirely due to hard work and application. She succeeded well, and when the long-awaited envelope dropped through the letter box one August morning, she was able to kiss her mother with a smile and pass her father the piece of paper that announced that she had gained three passes - two B's and a C in geography, history and English.

They were so thrilled that their joy almost made Iona weep, and they all three went out that evening for a celebratory dinner at the local hotel. As they munched their way through the warm prawn cocktail, tasteless fillets of plaice and sickly Black Forest gateau, Iona looked at her parents and her heart turned over in despair. They were both so utterly dear and dull, and she knew that she would be trapped forever in their sticky web of devotion.

Release came suddenly, in a shocking and unwanted way when, three years after the celebratory dinner, Iona's parents were killed in a car crash. They had gone to visit a friend in hospital, not eight miles away, when their car was sliced in two at a crossroads by a runaway lorry. They died instantly in the tangled wreck, but by the time Iona was called to identify them their mutilated bodies had been largely restored to respectability and when the green sheet was drawn reverently back to reveal their still, dead faces, they looked much as they had in life. The only thing missing was her father's pipe.

Iona's grief was profound, as she had never envisaged life without them. The small irritations that their suffocating adoration had on occasions provoked had been easily dealt with by her patent placebo of retreating into her fantasy world. Here she would weave her problems into the current romantic flight of fancy.

She had never thought about her own death or had a close association with anyone who had died, yet suddenly, her own immortality was in question. Iona found it impossible to believe that the two cold bodies that had once been her parents were no more than dust and ashes and that she too would one day be the same. There seemed little point in being a good and useful person when the inevitable end was so sudden and total. Even the ugly red brick of 28 Parkend Road was more enduring than the human beings that it sheltered.

Iona's parents seemed diminished by death and as the two coffins trundled towards the flames of the local crematorium, she wondered whether they tipped the bodies out and recycled the coffins.

As the small congregation drifted slowly away from the left-over sandwiches and tepid tea which Iona had provided for the wake, Mr Jones senior of Jones, Barraclough and Jones, solicitors, remained behind to acquaint Iona with what he referred to as the business aspect of her parents' death.

He called her *my dear* and asked if he might have something a bit stronger than tea before they settled to the reading of the will. Iona hunted in the small cupboard where her father had kept a modest reserve of alcohol and found a bottle of whisky. With an unexpected surge of defiance, Iona poured herself a small measure before offering the solicitor the bottle to help himself. She had never tasted spirits before and the amber liquid made her gasp as it burned its way down her throat.

Somewhere outside a Salvation Army band was playing *Onward Christian Soldiers* and as the drab, stuffy little room closed in on her and Mr Jones' voice droned on, Iona's life swam before her eyes and reality floated out of the window and away down the road to mingle with the strains of the band.

Unknown to Iona and, she suspected, her mother, Arthur Cridland had, as a result of shrewd investment and strict frugality, amassed a considerable amount of money. She had never thought about money and it was certainly not a subject that was mentioned in Parkend Road. The property itself was unencumbered and her father's investment portfolio sound and lucrative. The runaway lorry had left Iona a woman of independent means.

Darkness arrived and with the departure of Mr Jones and the Salvation Army, so did the return of Iona's predicament. She poured herself another drink and sat down to ponder on her situation and find a way through the jungle of her mind. There were no knights in shining armour to help her this time; no glorious young interns or bronzed boatmen.

She knew instinctively that the passage of her life would be a betrayal of her parent's devotion and of all that they valued, but a greater power would submerge her guilt. With this epiphany came liberation, and as dusk moved into night, the whisky went down and Iona drifted into sleep.

She awoke with the dawn feeling stiff, cold and rancid. The back of her head thumped, but her spirits sang in tune with the dusty sparrows who chattered their way into another day.

Her second birth was as swift and untroubled as her first, but this time the future lay within her own grasp. Now she had the power. The power to choose her own destiny.

*

'Hello, Jones, Barraclough & Jones? Could I speak to Mr Basil Jones please, it's Iona Cridland.'

'I'm putting you through now Miss Cridland' replied the telephonist in a bored voice, whilst continuing to file her nails.

'Good morning Iona, Basil Jones speaking. How can I

help you?'

'Morning Mr Jones,' *how could she ever call him Basil,* 'I thought I should tell you that I've put Parkend Road on the market. The agents tell me there should be no problem selling it – then I'm going to rent somewhere in the country. My aim is to buy, but I thought renting would give me a chance to see if I like country life before committing myself. When my parents' estate is settled, I would be most grateful if you would tell me exactly how much money I've got and how it's invested.'

She spoke quickly and firmly, anticipating protestations and interruptions from the staid solicitor.

'But my dear Iona,' he stuttered, 'are you quite sure I mean your job… your father would have… I must say...'

Iona cut him short.

'I've made up my mind, Mr Jones. In fact I've already given in my notice and have spoken to an agent in Wiltshire about renting a suitable property. I appreciate your concern but please don't worry about me. I have thought everything through and this is what I want to do.'

'Well Iona, I can only say that I am not at all happy with this wild scheme of yours, and with your late parents being such old friends of mine I feel rather responsible. However, if you have set your heart on this, I can only wish you well and assure you that I shall continue to guide and advise you should you require me to do so.'

'I appreciate that very much Mr Jones, but as I said, don't worry about me. I'm not a child and I'm not acting on the spur of the moment. I'll keep you posted. Goodbye for now.'

Iona slapped the handset back on its cradle and laughed out loud. *Poor old Basil, perhaps he harboured a secret desire to ditch his worthy wife and clutch of lumpy children and run away with Iona and her fortune to a desert island. What a thought!*

Iona wandered around the house that had been her

home for the 21 years that made up her life. She felt no sadness at the prospect of leaving it, only a twinge of remorse that she cared so little.

She picked up a photograph of her parents which her mother had given her one Christmas long ago. They were standing in front of an ancient abbey and underneath, her mother had written *Iona*. She supposed they must have got a fellow tourist to take this souvenir of their life together and as she held the tarnished silver frame, Iona felt the significance of this relic from the past. Her birth had made a point to her parents' otherwise pointless existence; her life their legacy to the continuation of mankind. 'And what will my point be I wonder,' she said aloud to the silent faces, 'what shall I leave behind?'

Iona had resolved to keep nothing from Parkend Road. She wanted a second life, uncluttered by reminders of her first. The way for her lay forward, not back, but something compelled her to place the photograph with the small pile of personal possessions that would accompany her to Wiltshire, her decision a subconscious surrendering to the impossibility of total severance from all that had shaped her.

Her plans progressed smoothly and the road ahead opened clear and straight. The small firm of chartered accountants where she had spent her working life gave her a modest farewell party and a whip-round produced a china shepherdess, chosen with great care to represent her new life amongst the sheep of Wiltshire. Iona was grateful for their kindness and friendship but she knew they were unable to comprehend her plans for the future and thought her quite mad.

She left Parkend Road without a backward glance, the Volkswagen she had recently bought easily able to accommodate her luggage. As she turned off the M4 and drove on through Hungerford and Marlborough an overwhelming sense of delight gripped her and she pressed her foot down on the accelerator pedal. Suddenly she couldn't wait to get to Bridge Cottage where at last she could start her new life – a life where there would be room for Max.

Max had come into Iona's life some years ago when she had gone to the cinema with a girlfriend. He was the personification of all that she had ever dreamed of, and his perfect Aryan face had filled the screen as he lived and loved his way through two hours of the Second World War.

Max was not a Nazi, he was a Prussian aristocrat and a loyal German member of the Wehrmacht who fought for his country but abhorred the little Austrian corporal. He was *simpatico* and glorious and he turned Iona's blood to water. She returned to the cinema alone and watched the film twice more and Max had stayed with her ever since.

Bridge Cottage, situated in a small village nestling in the foot of the Marlborough Downs, was everything that Iona had hoped it would be. She loved it from the beginning and had no hesitation in paying the asking price without quibble when, four months after the start of her tenancy, the owners decided to sell.

The sale of Parkend Road was completed without trouble and a letter from Basil Jones informed her that the financial side of her life was in good order provided she lived sensibly and her investments continued to prosper.

After their initial suspicion, the local people found nothing wrong with the new owner of Bridge Cottage, for Iona kept herself and her ideas to herself but was always friendly and pleasant when their paths crossed.

Her parents stared out of the silver frame and Iona was almost sure that their hitherto expression of stolid well-being had changed to one of disapproval and astonishment. Max stayed close by her side.

Iona was working in her garden when she heard the telephone ring. The garden had been neglected by the previous owners and it was hard work but she enjoyed it and the interruption annoyed her.

The invasion had succeeded and the German army occupied most of southern England. The Area Commandant had set up his HQ in the Manor House and Max had been billeted at Bridge Cottage. A German soldier had been shot by the locals and reprisals had been severe with three men executed and a group of young women rounded up and sent to the brothel the Nazis had established in the local town. But Max had saved Iona from this humiliating fate by pretending he wanted her for himself and she had become his servant. He had not touched her of course but he expected her to work hard and it was on his orders that she was digging the garden.

The bell went on ringing so Iona downed tools and ran in to answer it, the thread of her fantasy broken.

'Iona? Hi, it's Jenny, Jenny Percival.'

'Oh hello Jenny, how's things with you?'

Iona liked Jenny who was bright and uncomplicated and they had become good friends.

'I'm fine thanks – now don't say no before I've begun but the Young Farmers are having a dance at Dick Stafford's place on Saturday week and I'm getting up a party. There are a couple of spare blokes and I'd love you to come. It's very informal and good fun – do say yes.'

Iona hesitated, her immediate reaction being to decline the invitation but Jenny's insistence was hard to resist and anyway, why not go?

'Goodness Jenny, you've caught me on the hop but yes, I'd love to come and thank you for asking me.'

'Great, I'll tick your name and be in touch nearer the time with details. Bye for now and see you soon.'

From then on Iona began to drift into the life of the small rural community. An endless round of fund raising functions for the church, the sports ground and the village school kept most of the ladies busy while their menfolk toiled on the land. There were others too, and the village boasted an aspiring author, a retired brigadier, a city slicker who only appeared at weekends, and an antique dealer who had a shop in the local town.

Once a year, a sponsored Ride in aid of the air ambulance was hosted by the village pub. It was a new experience for Iona who found it a good spirited affair, with a glass of port and chunk of delicious fruit cake for all. Jenny was there on her horse and called out a greeting to Iona as she trotted past when the riders set off down the road.

'Yes,' she said to the birds as she wandered back to Bridge Cottage, 'I like this life. It's as if I've never been anywhere else.'

'Morning Ronnie,' she greeted the postman, 'you're late today. Anything for me?'

'Yes Miss, a letter from the big city by the looks of things.'

'Thanks, see you.'

Iona hung up her coat and made a cup of coffee before picking up the letter. She saw it was from Jones, Barraclough & Jones and felt inclined to ignore it until she felt more in the mood for tedious paperwork. It was probably nothing important anyway. Perhaps she had better read it now and get shot of it.

My dear Iona, the letter began, *I trust this letter finds you in good health and continuing to enjoy your life in the country.*

Whilst in no way wishing to alarm you, I feel it my duty to draw to your attention the current position with regard to your finances. Last year, some of your investments did not yield the dividends that I expected, and it has been brought to my notice that your personal expenditure has increased considerably.

As I said, there is no cause for alarm as yet and obviously we shall continue to manage your affairs with your best interests in mind. In the light of this information however, I feel that you will wish to plan your personal spending with a little more care and perhaps consider seeking some form of employment to supplement your income.

The letter finished with the usual best wishes and Iona scrumpled it up and threw it at the rubbish bin but it hit the edge and bounced back onto the floor. She got up to rescue it when she heard a horse in the yard outside the kitchen and a voice calling.

'Iona, are you there? It's me.'

'What on earth are you doing back already Jenny, I thought you always stayed out till the bitter end.'

Jenny's coat was filthy, and the horse's knees bloody.

'Oh dear, things gone a bit wrong?'

'Yes, he slipped up on the concrete in old Brookshaw's cattle yard. Look at the state of my coat, covered in cow muck. Can I hose his legs then phone Phil to bring the lorry? He's lame and it won't do him any good to walk all the way back to the farm.'

'Of course you can. Do you want some Dettol or something?'

'No thanks, cold hosing will do fine for now and I'll do him up properly when he's home. Phil shouldn't be long but have you got an old rug I could chuck over him, I don't want him getting cold.'

'Will do – and I'll put the kettle on.'

By the time Iona had dug out a blanket, Jenny had finished her ministrations and tied the well-behaved animal up in the yard.

'Fancy a cup of tea?' Iona asked her friend when she came back from telephoning.

'Not half! Particularly if it's got a drop of whisky in it.'

'No problem, sit down and I'll get it. Are you OK by the way, no broken bones or anything?'

'No I'm fine thanks, a bruise or two but nothing to get

excited about. Who's been missing the rubbish bin then?' Jenny picked up the paper ball that was Basil Jones's letter.

'Oh that, you'd better read it. Seems I'm on hard times.'

Jenny smoothed out the crumpled paper to read the offending letter whilst drinking her tea with appreciative gulps.

'Well, it doesn't sound too bad. Got any more tea? I bet your Basil Jones is a real old scaremonger stick-in-the-mud type.'

'Help yourself to the brown stuff. He is all those things but I suppose he might have a point. What do you think I should do? I couldn't possibly go and get some awful boring office job. That's partly what I ran away from and I've forgotten how to type anyway.'

'Well, let's think. You could ... I know, I've had a brainwave. Marry Henry Barton, he's got pots of money and is desperate to find a wife!'

'Jenny, you really are mad! He's as old as the hills and looks like a boiled beetroot. Thanks a lot but you'll have to come up with something better than that!'

'Actually, I have got a serious thought. Why don't you think about doing B & B? You've got plenty of room and you could keep most of the money away from the tax man.'

'That might not be such a bad idea – worth thinking about anyway. I'm not too bad a cook, and if I didn't like the look of the people I could tell them I'm full. It might shut old Basil up for a year or two.'

A hooting horn announced the arrival of the lorry and Jenny jumped up to rescue her stricken steed.

'Better go, thanks Iona and see you soon.'

'Bye Jenny and hope the horse is OK. I'll give you a ring.'

The lorry roared away and Iona was left to her thoughts.

She rather liked the bed and breakfast idea and decided to investigate the enterprise further. An inspection of the house would be a good start. Bridge Cottage had been built originally as two small dwellings for farm workers, but had long ago been sold off and made into one. As the land had gone under the plough, so had manpower given way to machinery and the era of the tied cottage come to an end.

As Iona walked around the house, she thought about the people whose lives had been lived under this same roof. Their joys and sorrows and the whole tapestry of human life that must have been witnessed by these four walls. There was little evidence left of their existence, yet once they had been significant, and it seemed sad to Iona that now they might as well never have been.

It will be the same for me, she thought. *In 100 years time, I shall just be another name on the deeds, a faceless person who left nothing behind. Perhaps I might spend the winter unearthing the history of the cottages and those who lived here and then add my own chapter.*

She liked the idea of writing a nicely presented history which would stay with the house and be updated by each successive incumbent. What fascinating reading it would make for future inhabitants.

Iona came out of the past and back to the present with the realisation that a certain amount of work would be needed before she could get the B & B scheme under way. There would be a bit more involved than just hanging up a sign.

She went back downstairs to the kitchen and settled down with pen and paper. She made a list of all the things she thought necessary for her new venture; advertising, bath towels, easy care sheets and a chat with Mrs Marsh who kept the village stores and knew everything about anything.

The way was clear and on impulse she picked up the

telephone and dialled Jenny's number.

'Jenny, hello, it's me, Iona. I'm going to go for it, the B & B thing. Just thought I'd ring to tell you and to check everything's OK after your confrontation with Brookshaw's concrete.'

'Yes fine thanks. Jack's all wrapped up, anti-bioticated and munching his dinner and Phil and I are about to munch ours. Great news about becoming a landlady – you realise you must have fat, rosy cheeks and a large white apron to wipe your floury hands on as you bake the bread, and by the way, if you need lessons on how to produce an English breakfast, apply to me – I do it every day!'

'I will, don't worry,' laughed Iona. 'But I won't be opening up till Easter so I've got plenty of time to learn.'

'Bye for now and don't forget you promised to come to old Ma Lambert's wretched coffee morning next week – it's in aid of defrocked clergymen or something equally thrilling.'

Life was good; there was no doubt about it. So good in fact that there had hardly been time for Max. Luckily he had been allowed back to Germany on leave, to visit his mother who was old and sick and Iona had hardly missed him at all.

*

Winter dragged on and Iona made preparations for her debut as a Bed & Breakfast landlady the following spring. She also began the history of Bridge Cottage and its past inhabitants, helped by local chat, the parish register and the public library.

Max had returned from Germany and was having problems with his C.O. – a hard-line Nazi who treated the locals with arrogant contempt and was keener on shooting them than trying to establish cordial relations. He returned each night feeling depressed, his personal beliefs in conflict with his job. He liked Iona to dine with him so that he could relax and converse with a *normal human being* as he put it, like he used to do at home in Germany before it all began. After dinner though, the master/servant relationship returned and they went their separate ways.

March came, and spring pushed steadily forward, struggling against an unusually late fall of snow. Iona visited the local Tourist Information Centre and registered on the list of accommodation, and as Easter approached, she hung her new sign at the end of the drive. Now all that remained was for the customers to roll in.

It was a glorious summer, and with the pound weak against the European currencies, overseas visitors were plentiful. Iona found herself much busier than she had anticipated, and although the money was good, the work involved was much harder than she had imagined it would be. By mid-August she was fed up with making beds, washing sheets, and being nice to total strangers who all too often seemed to find something trivial to complain about. Her house was no longer her own, and by the end of the summer holidays she felt exhausted and the once hoped for scrunch of tyres on the gravel became an unwanted imposition.

'Think of all that lovely money,' said Jenny, 'and keeping old Basil quiet!'

'Oh! I know Jenny, but it's such a drag I can't tell you – pregnant sheep and bellowing cows must be heaven compared to this job.'

'Why not shut up shop then? Take the sign down and if anyone rings, tell them you've got swine fever or something, after all you've done well for a first effort.'

'Yes, I think I will actually. I could do with a break and a chance to catch up on other things. See you soon.'

Iona sat down and gave a sigh of relief. Jenny was right, she had done well and the income had covered her modest summer expenditure.

She walked down the drive to take down the sign

which she stowed away in the garden shed. *Perhaps I shall be keen again by the time next spring comes around,* she thought, as she meandered back into the silent house.

A few days later, as she was changing to go to a barbecue, the telephone rang. A heavily accented male voice very much hoped that there would be a room available for five nights at the end of September. He would be no trouble he assured her, for he would be out all day working on a research project and would not require a cooked breakfast, only toast and coffee.

Iona hesitated, her mind far away from B & B. Sensing her hesitation, he assured her again that he would be most grateful and trouble free. As she was already late for the barbeque and couldn't see any real reason not to have him, she agreed. After all, it was good money when the same sheets did five days and no bacon was required.

By the time Iona arrived, the party was in full swing and she spotted Jenny amongst the crowd gathered round the hog roast.

'Guess what, I've just booked a man in for five nights at the end of the month and that really is going to be my final effort. I think I might have a party to celebrate and spend some of my hard-gotten gains – I do owe quite a few people.'

'Sounds a great idea to me, the party I mean, but do you think you ought to have an unknown man alone in the house with you? He might be a sex maniac. Let me know if he's a stunner and I'll be round to help with the bed making.'

'He's probably 90 and hideous – and I'm sure he's fine. He sounded very polite and foreign, and he's researching the history of various English country villages – just your type, Jenny!'

'Thanks a lot. Come on, I can see Phil peering down that blond tart's cleavage – she sure makes the most of her tits. Let's go and put a spanner in his lust and get a top-up on the way.'

The evening was a success and Iona woke the next morning with a dry mouth and a headache. Her parents gazed disapprovingly out of their frame and as she swallowed black coffee and paracetamol, her mind turned back over her life. She remembered her school friends and the graphic accounts of their early sexual encounters and her own decision to preserve her virginity for Mr. Right. *But when would he appear*, she wondered? She had enjoyed herself last night and knew there was no shortage of men who would have taken her to bed had she wished it. She liked them and found them amusing company, but had no desire to gratify their lust. Max had ruined that for her. Max was perfect and nothing less would do.

Autumn came early that year and the harvest had been good and easy. As the last of the corn trailers roared through the village, carrying their loads to the silos, Iona set about tidying up the garden and preparing for winter. She enjoyed the recognition of the changing seasons that country people bestowed on the year. It was not something that urban life had acknowledged in the same way.

Suddenly it was the end of September and Iona had forgotten all about her last B & B booking. He was due to arrive in two days' time, and as she prepared the room and laid in some extra supplies, she wondered what he would be like and where he was from. She had little ability to differentiate between foreign accents but she did, by now, understand continental number plates.

When a car arrived on time two days later, Iona looked out of the window and saw that it was German. As she ran downstairs, the front door knocker banged and she opened the door. Her heart jumped into her mouth, for there on the doorstep stood Max.

For a moment, she was unable to speak. The man stared down at her, a look of surprise in the blue, Aryan eyes: 'Perhaps I have not the correct house but I look for Miss Cridland,' his English was careful and heavily accented. I am Helmuth von Arnsberg.'

'Yes, no, I mean I'm so sorry, you are in the right place. How do you do, I am Iona Cridland.'

'I think perhaps you forget that I come?' he smiled, bowing slightly and taking her outstretched hand.

'No, I had not forgotten and please do come in. Would you like a cup of tea now or would you prefer to get settled in first?'

'You are most kind and I should like very much some English tea before I place my luggage.'

The German sat watching her as she fussed unnecessarily with the simple preparations for tea, before allowing his gaze to travel over the room, his eyes expressionless as he observed the Englishness of it all. He hated the English with their easy self-assurance and misplaced belief in their superiority.

His mother had been English, his beautiful, loving mother who had called him her little German sausage and abandoned him when he was four years old. All evidence of her had been removed from his father's house and she was never spoken of again. He had cried for days, but the nurse had reprimanded him and his stern, distant father told him that he was a German. He must remember that and forget his unfortunate mother. Gradually his heart had darkened and his bitterness turned on the instrument of his grief.

It had taken years to trace his mother's family, and to discover that they had once lived in this unimportant little Wiltshire village.

Iona put the tea on the table. 'Help yourself to milk and sugar, and when you've finished, I'll show you your room and where everything is. I seldom lock the house so you can come and go as you please and if you get bored with the local pub food, I'm quite happy to do an evening meal provided I have some warning.'

'Thank you Miss Cridland,' he smiled his charming smile, 'I am certain I shall be most happy to be here.'

Herr von Arnsberg settled in quickly and easily and within two days of visiting the local pub for his supper, was asking Iona if he might take up her offer of home cooking.

She acquiesced eagerly, her emotions almost uncontrollable as the personification of her fantasy took hold of her existence. Every aspect of the forthcoming dinner was a matter of great concern, not least her own appearance and she worked all day to produce the perfect evening. Here was Max at last, literally landed on the doorstep.

The dinner was a success and the German never considered going to the pub again. On his fourth night he asked if he might stay a little longer as he enjoyed the area and was in no particular hurry to return home. Iona was sure that in reality he wanted to stay because of her. An unseen current seemed to flow between them, the *coup de foudre* of romantic novels, and she awaited his next move.

It came the next day when he suggested that, in return for her kindness, he would like to have the honour of taking her out to dinner if she could suggest somewhere suitable to go.

'What a lovely idea!' Iona agreed happily. 'We'll go to the Rising Sun – it's not far and the food's good. We shouldn't be too late though as it gets busy on a Friday and can be rather rowdy later on.'

'Ah Fraulein Cridland, your English pubs are what you call an institution I think, always with the many ornaments and the noisy young men.'

Iona laughed. 'Do call me Iona, Fraulein sounds a bit odd and Miss Cridland makes me feel like an old spinster school mistress.'

'I shall be honoured and you may call me Helmuth and then we are, how do you say, quits?'

'Very good,' Iona commended his idiomatic English.

'But would you think it very strange if I was to call you Max? It is a rather odd request but Max has always been my idea of a splendid German name whereas Helmuth rather reminds me of an old tin hat!'

Her heart thumped as she made her strange request - *I must have gone mad* she thought.

A flash of irritation crossed the German's face but was swiftly gone as he smiled and gave his inevitable little bow.

'It is strange that you should ask this unusual thing of me for I have Maximilian for a name also, and so you see it will be quite proper for you to call me Max if so you wish.'

'There! What did I tell you!' cried Iona, 'a real German name – that's great – Max you shall be.'

At that moment the telephone rang and as Iona went to answer it, Max said he would be going out for a bit but would not be late back. Iona waved as she picked up the telephone. It was Jenny.

'How are you getting on with the dashing Kraut, does he click his heels and live off cabbage and wurst for breakfast!' she giggled.

'Don't be silly Jenny,' Iona replied sharply. 'He eats toast and marmalade and is taking me to the Rising Sun for dinner tonight.'

'Ooh I say, perhaps he fancies you – look out, he's probably got a fat Frau and 10 kinder tucked away in the good old Farterland.'

'Honestly Jenny, you do talk some rot sometimes. Actually, he's charming and I'm really looking forward to spending the evening with someone who can think beyond corn prices and cow muck.'

'Sorry Iona, I was only pulling your leg. Look, I've got

to dash but have good dins and be careful. You don't know anything about him and I'd hate to see you get hurt. I'll ring in the morning for an update.'

'Thanks Jen and bye for now.'

Iona was sorry she had been sharp with her friend who she knew meant well, but nothing, nothing at all would come between her and Max. She knew instinctively that the long-awaited conclusion of her fantasy was about to become reality, and that Max was the one she had kept herself for.

It was late afternoon when Iona decided to begin her preparations for the forthcoming evening by washing her hair and selecting the clothes she would wear. She wanted to look casual but attractive and feminine and as her wardrobe was rather limited, it would take some time to select the ideal combination.

As she went upstairs, she found herself heading for Max's room, which was at the opposite end of the house from hers. The temptation to be amongst his things was too great to resist and she longed to find out more about the private man. Jenny had been right, she knew very little about him for he seemed to have a desire to keep their conversations on a very general level and away from himself. The room revealed little until she opened a drawer and found his passport. As she read the first page, a shock went through her. His name was not Helmuth Maximilian von Arnsberg but Gunther Fernau. Her hands trembled as she replaced the passport, and she was on her way downstairs to ring Jenny when she heard his car pull into the yard. Too late.

I shall probe a bit at dinner, she thought as she lay in the bath, *it'll be easier in the relaxed atmosphere of the restaurant.*

The Rising Sun did not let Iona down and by the time Max ordered coffee, she had forgotten all about his mysterious identity. He had been his most charming self and she was conquered. Whoever he was and whatever he was doing no longer mattered as she basked in the glow of her passion. As they left, he took her arm and handed her into his car. It was the first time he had touched her and she experienced a feeling she had never known before. It was a kind of tightening in what her mother might have called the nether regions, and a strange prickling all over her skin.

When they returned to Bridge Cottage, Iona offered Max a nightcap but he declined, saying he was tired and would go straight up to bed. But it had been a wonderful evening he told her, and as he kissed her hand, his eyes spoke of other things.

After Max had gone upstairs, Iona poured herself a small whisky. She had drunk sparingly at dinner, not wanting to let any degree of inebriation overtake her. As the whisky burned down her throat, she remembered the night of her parent's funeral when she had sampled the drink for the first time.

Was she really the same Iona Cridland who had lived at number 28 Parkend Road for all those years? It was impossible to believe that she must be. She raised her glass to the photograph of her parents, appreciating for the first time their creation of her. Now her life would have a purpose, and she too might leave more behind than the history of Bridge Cottage.

She emptied her glass and went upstairs to begin her preparations for bed. She was sure he would come to her room and she wanted everything to be as she had always imagined it should be for the great moment in her life. Beyond that she never looked.

Iona was glad she had drunk the whisky, as after vigourously brushing her teeth to remove any trace of the smell, she felt more relaxed and climbed into bed feeling excited and confident.

She must have fallen into a light sleep, for when Max

came in, she did not hear the door open. The light from the passage shone through her bedroom door as he stood beside the bed, smiling down at her.

Now that the time had come, Iona had no idea what to say or do. She watched in fascination as the German undid the bathrobe he was wearing, revealing his naked body as it fell to the floor. As he climbed into bed beside her, his expression changed and he began muttering strange German words that she did not understand. He rolled on top of her, forcing her legs apart with his knees, all tenderness and consideration vanished. Surely this was not what she had waited so long for?

As he forced himself into her, Iona cried out and tried to resist but he clamped his hand over her mouth, pinning her back onto the pillows so she was unable to move. The torrent of German words turned to laughter as his hands moved from her breasts and closed round her neck. She could not even scream and as she died, the fantasy died with her.

*

The autumn sun rose over Bridge Cottage and the birds began their morning song, as they always had done when Gunther Fernau's mother had listened to them as a child.

Downstairs the telephone rang, but there was nobody there to answer it. The silent Cridlands gazed out of their silver frame as a tractor roared past on its way to plough the stubble, ready for the autumn planting. The cycle of life had begun all over again.

BOOK THREE: THE SABOTEUR

The pony's hooves beat out a weary rhythm as it walked along the rain-drenched road; small splashes of water spurting up as each foot struck the surface with the hollow sound that comes from iron on wet tarmac.

The young girl in the saddle leant forward to pat its neck and murmur encouraging words. The pony flicked an ear in acknowledgment of her gesture, plodding steadily on towards its destination.

A small, bedraggled group of hunt saboteurs were also making their way home along the same road, their once bright placards now as wet and tired as the girl and the pony.

As they heard its hoof beats coming up behind them, they turned to jeer.

'Bloody murderer,' shouted a tall, thin girl who's long dark hair lay plastered round her angry face.

'Leave off, it's only a kid.'

'Hitler was only a kid once,' she sneered, and shook the remains of the placard she was carrying in the pony's face.

Shying away in alarm, it slipped on the smooth surface and, unable to keep its footing, fell sideways onto the road. The girl was thrown heavily towards the grass verge and her head cracked onto the concrete surround of a drain. The pony scrambled up, and seeming unsure about what to do next, moved onto the verge and lowered its head to eat. The girl lay still.

'You idiot, now look what you've done,' cried a frightened looking youth, 'we'd better get help.'

'Fuck that for starters, I'm getting out of here. Who cares anyway, she got what she deserves, the murdering little bitch,' spat the dark girl.

'Come on mate, she's right, this could mean trouble.'

The worried youth hesitated for a moment, before turning away and following his companions as they ran off up the road towards their van.

The pony raised its head and looked after them as they disappeared round a corner and out of sight. Then it resumed its grazing.

*

'Isn't Lucy back yet Mum? She promised I could use her PC and I've got Frank Harvey's new football game thing, it's brilliant...'

'Goodness Ben,' said Mary Cardew, looking up from her desk as her son came into the room. 'I've lost all track of the time with these wretched IACS forms and the movement orders. She should be back by now.'

'Can I use it anyway, I know she wouldn't mind.'

'No love, better not. You know how private she is about her room these days. She's a teenager now and teenagers can be a bit funny about things. Three years from now and you'll be just the same.'

'Oh *pleeze* Mum,' wheedled Ben, giving his mother his most winning 10 year-old smile. But her mind was on his sister, and his efforts were ignored.

'Run out to the stables for me and see if Lucy's back. Where's your father?'

'Milking of course. When I get back, can I use....'

'Ben, just do as I say – now.'

'OK, OK.'

Mary ran a hand through her short, chestnut brown hair and turned once more to the forms on which she was working. Her concentration broken, she abandoned her work and thought about her son. Ben Cardew was more interested in football and cars than older sisters or school work. He was nearly always in the bottom half of his form at the local Middle School that he attended, but he was well-behaved enough to be liked by his teachers, and naughty enough to be popular with his peers. He was a cheerful, uncomplicated boy, and neither Mary nor her husband Ted had ever worried too much about their son's future. They had always assumed that he would follow in his father's footsteps, and one day take over the farm.

Mary sighed, and wondered whether they were doing the right thing by encouraging the boy along this path. It was hard to make a decent living on the land, and there were few grounds for optimism at the moment.

Mary looked around the old familiar walls that had seen so much of the life of the Cardew family, and wondered whether her son's son would ever sit in this chair, and experience that good feeling of continuity and purpose that she valued so highly.

Ben's reappearance broke her train of thought.

'Lucy's not back,' he said, 'Dad says to ring up Mrs Vicary 'cos she's probably gone home with Poppy.'

Poppy Vicary was Lucy's best friend, and the two girls usually went hunting together. The Vicarys had come from London, and Mary liked them both. Sally and Derek had pitched into country life with enthusiasm and open-mindedness and Mary enjoyed hearing about their former life, which had been so different to hers.

After one school term of friendship with Lucy, all Poppy had aspired to was to learn to ride and be able to join her friend in Pony Club activities, as well as the excitement of going out hunting. She had taken to it like a duck to water and, with the full support of her parents, had quickly become a competent horsewoman with a pony of her own.

Mary and Sally both preferred the girls to ride together when out hunting, in case anything went wrong and one of them needed help. Their local hunt was a small, friendly pack where children were made welcome and were well looked after, but there were occasions when, for some reason or another, they could find themselves on their own. The two mothers felt much happier if the girls kept each other company.

Ben's words filtered through to Mary's brain, *Lucy not back when she should be, ring the Vicarys*. 'Thanks Ben, I think I will. It's not like Lucy to stay out so late without getting word back to us.'

'She said she wouldn't be late as Pickles was tired after Saturday,' added Ben. 'It's jolly mean of her when she knows I want to use her PC.'

Mary smiled at her frowning son, her hazel eyes shut briefly as anxiety for her daughter's safety crept into her soul.

'Go and feed the dogs Ben, could you, while I phone the Vicarys – there's a new bag of food in the store if you need it and don't forget to give Squirt his pill.'

She knew the number by heart, and as she punched the buttons on the telephone, she found herself silently praying that her husband was right and that Lucy was with her friend.

'Hello,' a young girl's voice answered.

'Oh hello Poppy, it's Mrs Cardew, is Lucy with you?'

'No, she isn't – she should be home by now though. We split at Stackman's Cross as usual ages ago. We left before the last draw as we were soaked and it'd been a bum day anyway.'

'Was Pickles all right, not lame or lost a shoe or anything?'

'No, he was fine and Lucy said she was looking forward to getting home to a hot bath and tea. Shall I call Mum?'

'Yes please Poppy, I'll just have a quick word.'

The receiver clattered down and Mary heard Poppy's voice in the background, shouting for her mother. Her hand suddenly felt clammy on the handset as her heart thumped in her chest.

'Mary, what's this about Lucy not being home?'

'Oh Sally, I'm so worried. Poppy said she should have

been home some time ago. I was doing those blasted IACS forms and lost all track of the time. Whatever can have happened?'

'Don't panic Mary, I'm sure there's some perfectly reasonable explanation – Lucy's a very sensible girl.'

'I know – maybe she's come in while we've been talking – I'll nip out to the stable.'

'Keep me posted won't you Mary, and for heaven's sake ring if there's anything we can do.'

'Of course and thanks Sally. Bye for now.'

Mary replaced the receiver and stood for a moment, breathing deeply and trying to stem the rising tide of panic that threatened to drown her. *Sally is right* she reasoned, *keep calm, there must be a perfectly good explanation,* but alongside these thoughts flashed images of her daughter: Lucy, neat and serious, winning rosettes at the local gymkhana; Lucy laughing with Ben on the roundabout at the village funfair, her fair hair ruffled and blowing into her cornflower blue eyes, her creamy young skin flushed pink with excitement.

Stop it, stop it.

She ran to the milking parlour, wishing they could afford to replace the outdated equipment that cost Ted so much time and aggravation in breakdowns.

He had nearly finished scraping down the parlour floor and was looking forward to his tea when his wife came in.

'Hello love,' he smiled, easing his tired back, but the smile quickly faded when he noticed that his wife's normally serene and contented face looked tight and worried.

'What's up then?' he asked, imagining some tedious domestic problem.

'It's Lucy, Ted. She's not back from hunting and I've just spoken to Sally. Poppy said she should have been home ages ago. Something's wrong, Ted, she's in trouble.'

Ted put down the scraper and went at once to where

his wife stood in the doorway.

'Come on then, we'll go and look for her – this can wait for once. What did Poppy say?'

'She said they parted at Stackman's Cross and Lucy took the back lane as usual. They left before the last draw and there was nothing wrong with Pickles. Oh Ted, whatever can have happened?'

'I don't know love, but the first thing to do is to drive to the Cross by the lane and then round the block the main road way. Something may have made her change her mind and go back for some reason. Go and tell Ben what's up and to listen for the phone, I expect he's glued to that wretched television. I'll get the truck.'

Mary ran back into the house, her heart thumping with the dread that gripped her. She slowed to a walk in the hall, forcing herself to appear calm in front of her son. As predicted by Ted, Ben was watching television.

'Ben, Dad and I are going to look for Lucy in case Pickles's gone lame or something. Listen out for the phone could you, we won't be long.'

'OK Mum,' he replied, without taking his eyes off the screen.

The old Toyota pickup was revving up in the yard, clouds of black, smelly diesel fumes belching from the exhaust.

Mary grabbed an old horse blanket that was lying in a heap of clutter on the boiler room floor and dashed through the rain to jump in beside Ted.

Neither of them spoke as they drove slowly along the narrow lane that Lucy should have taken for the hack home. The dirty November night had already closed in, and the headlights of the truck were full on. As they rounded a bend, the bright beams suddenly caught the shape of a pony in their path.

'It's Pickles,' cried Mary, clutching Ted's arm as he slowed to a stop. She was out of the truck before he had switched off the engine, and quickly caught the bemused looking animal who seemed relieved to see someone whose voice was familiar.

Green slime dribbled out of its mouth where a clod of grass had become wound round the bit. It was unable to chew properly as, at Mary's insistence, it always wore a Grackle noseband when hunting to keep its mouth shut and give Lucy more control.

'Look Ted, he's grazed his off-side hip and fetlock joint. He must have slipped somehow and come down on the road.'

Ted looked the pony over and nodded in agreement, frowning.

'It doesn't make sense though, Lucy knows this lane is slippery in places and she's much too sensible to take silly chances – she always walks down here.'

'Oh Ted I know, but his shoes were quite worn. He should have been shod last week but I thought we could squeeze a few more days out of the old set and get through half-term.'

'Tie him to the truck – here, I'll get some baler twine and the big torch and we'll walk the rest of the lane up to the Cross.'

Mary knew now that her initial fears were well-founded, for Lucy would never have abandoned her pony in this way unless she had been unable to do anything else.

Mary herself had been born and bred with horses and had brought her daughter up to understand the responsibility of horse ownership; the need to accept the inevitable disappointments that punctuated the hard work and pleasure, and to always put the welfare of the animal first.

She tied the pony to the Toyota where it stood watching them patiently as they set off on their lonely search up the black, vanishing lane.

They had gone nearly 200 yards before the shaft of light cast by the powerful torch picked out the still form of their daughter's body. Ted gave a short, low cry as they broke into a run, but Mary felt a strange numbness and a sense of unreality overcome her, as if this was all some nightmare from which she would shortly wake up.

'Oh my God, my God,' she whispered, bending over Lucy's still body. 'Her new hat, where's her hat?'

'Don't move her – she's alive. Look Mary, she's breathing.'

Suddenly, as the nightmare became reality, Mary's character reasserted itself and she became the calm, practical person that she was.

'There's a rug in the truck Ted – we must keep her warm – then go ring for the ambulance – *quick* – leave Pickles, he won't come to any harm.'

They clasped hands briefly before Ted turned and ran back to the truck, his big, gumbooted feet splashing on the lane as he desperately tried to force his normally steady stockman's legs to grow wings.

Mary knew she should have fetched the blanket herself for she was a small, wiry woman who had run for the county when she was a schoolgirl. It would have saved time, but somehow she could not bear to leave her daughter.

The truck roared back, Ted still breathing heavily from his run as they carefully wrapped the blanket round Lucy's prostrate body.

'Ring Sally too, she'll deal with Pickles – and Ben.' She suddenly remembered her son, sitting at home in front of the television, 'and hurry Ted, *please hurry.*'

Mary never looked at her watch, but it seemed as if an eternity had passed before she saw headlights coming down the lane.

'Hang on Lucy, hang on, we're here and Pickles is fine,' she said over and over again, and suddenly Ted was there, by her side again.

'Sally and Derek have come with me. Sally will take Pickles home and Derek can take the truck back to the farm, shut up the dogs, then fetch her and Ben back to their place. I said I would ring as soon as we have any news.'

'The ambulance …?'

'It's on its way, listen.'

The distant noise of the siren grew louder, and the blue light became visible as it flashed its menacing beam over the surrounding fields.

Mary's eyes were like black pits in her shrunken face as she lifted them in relief as the ambulance swished to a halt a few yards from where they stood. She took Ted's hand as the paramedics shouldered them aside with barely a murmur of sympathy.

They stood helplessly together in the rain, outsiders now in a tragedy beyond their control, as their daughter was loaded into the ambulance.

'We're coming too,' Mary cried in anguish as a uniformed man went to close the doors.

'Hop in then,' and he smiled and gave Mary his hand to help her up as Ted followed. He seemed more human than the others, but he got into the front with the driver and they were left alone while Lucy was taken away from them by the intent men with their grave faces and emergency equipment.

The hideous siren wailed on as they sped through the dark, temporarily cocooned from the outside world.

Nobody spoke to them and when they arrived at the hospital, Mary and Ted could do nothing but watch as Lucy's still unconscious body was wheeled through a pair of doors which shut with a swish behind her.

They were shown where to wait and offered cups of tea as an efficient woman with a clip board asked a multitude of questions. But the agony of waiting for news of Lucy dragged on.

The waiting room was empty and silent, and as the night wore on, Ted fell asleep. He had been up since 5.30 for morning milking and had missed his usual short after lunch sit-down because of problems with the machinery in the parlour.

What are they doing, why doesn't anyone come, why didn't I have Pickles shod. Oh God don't let her die. Jumbled thoughts raced round inside Mary's head until she thought she would go mad.

A lifetime later, the door of the dreary little room opened and a young doctor came in. A tall thin man, he looked tired and pale and a blue shadow showed on his sallow face.

'Mr. and Mrs. Cardew? I'm Dr Dawson.'

Mary and Ted rose anxiously to their feet, but he gestured to them to stay seated and sat down himself with a sigh, two chairs away from Mary, as if somehow wanting to distance himself from the personal aspect of the calamity.

'Your daughter has fractured her skull, which as I'm sure you are both aware, is a serious injury. The head is a very vulnerable part of the human body and should never be exposed to unnecessary risk.'

Mary winced at the man's implied criticism of their care of Lucy and a spark of anger rose above her distress.

'But we had just bought her a new approved riding hat, the best on the market. She was never allowed on the pony without it and I cannot understand how it came off.'

As he read the anguish in the parents' eyes, Dr Dawson relented a little before continuing.

'I'm sorry, it's been a long day and I shouldn't have said that. But so many accidents could be avoided if only people would take more care. Now, to return to young Lucy, she has suffered no other injuries and her condition is stable at the moment. However, she is still unconscious and what we would describe as being in a coma.'

The word *coma* made Mary gasp. She had read about people who had been like this and they had never come round; or else they had been left permanently disabled in some way.

Dr Dawson rattled a quick mental assessment of the woman through his tired brain, and decided that she and her nice looking husband were people who could take the truth without any flannel.

'We measure the depth of coma by something called the Glasgow coma score. This is a point system whereby response to external stimuli, the movement of the limbs and eyes are scored in a range from 3-15. Three being deep coma and 15 the normal level of consciousness. Lucy is on 7. The good news is that the MRI scan has shown no sign of a blood clot yet. In people of her age, what we call an extra-dural haemorrhage is the most common cause and usually occurs within a few hours of the blow to the head, so there is a good chance that bleeding will not occur. However, we cannot be certain for a day or so.'

'So you can't tell us any more at the moment then, doctor?' asked Ted.

'I'm afraid not, Mr Cardew. Prognosis is very uncertain in cases like this. The human brain is a very complicated mechanism, and a scan or electroencephalogram can only give us a fairly crude idea of what is really going on.'

'When can we see her?' asked Mary, her voice flat and emotionless.

'Come along tomorrow afternoon when we will have a better idea of how things are going. Of course we will telephone you immediately if there is any change, but for now the best thing you can do is go home and get some sleep. Lucy is in good hands, I can promise you that.'

'Thank you,' said Ted simply. 'Come on Mary, the doctor's right and we must think of Ben too.'

He took his wife's arm and guided her out of the hospital.

'Heavens, I've forgotten we haven't got a car – wait here while I phone for a taxi, won't be long.'

As Ted strode off to find a telephone, Mary gazed up at the night sky. The rain had stopped and the stars were beginning to shine through the clearing cloud. How vast and unfathomable the universe was; Mary could not comprehend infinity and she felt small and unimportant as she gazed heavenwards.

She thought of the other people all over the world who, too, must be suffering under those same stars, who at this very moment were dying, being born, having terrible accidents.

But now Lucy was her universe, Lucy and their small patch of the earth. That was all that mattered.

The taxi came quickly and took them back to their silent home. 'We must ring Sally and Derek. They said to keep them posted no matter what the time; they've got a phone by the bed. You brew us up a nice hot toddy while I do that then we'll obey doctor's orders and go to bed. The cows have still got to be milked!' Ted kissed his wife then headed for the office to make the call.

Mary put the kettle on the old *Rayburn* and went to find the whisky. They were not regular drinkers themselves, but being of a hospitable nature, Ted always kept a bottle of whisky and some wine in the cupboard for when friends came round and they could all enjoy a drink together.

She heard Ted's voice murmuring in the background and the click as he replaced the receiver. He came straight back into the kitchen and sank down in the old Windsor chair he liked so much, his normally cheerful face drawn and pale.

Mary handed him a steaming glass and took a sip from her own, burning her tongue in the process. 'How's Ben?'

she asked, feeling guilty that she had given so little thought to her son. Lucy was his sister after all, and beneath the sibling bickering lay a close bond.

'I spoke to Sally and she said Ben's fine, asleep in bed and he's been very good about it all. She's going to run him back in the morning and then we can tell him properly about Lucy.'

'I'm glad about that, poor Ben, it must be horrid for him, too, and being away from us and home. Did Sally say anything else?'

'They are all devastated of course, but Poppy has taken it very hard. Sally said she blames herself you see, because apparently when they were hacking home Lucy said her chin strap was rubbing and Poppy said why not undo it, she always did, then did it up again before she got home in case her mother saw.'

'Oh Ted, poor child, that's an awful cross to bear at thirteen. Even so, I still don't understand why Pickles slipped up even allowing for his shoes. He's such a sensible pony, and Lucy always walks the last two miles home from hunting. When we were children we never had crash helmets at all, just ordinary, useless old riding caps and we all survived.'

'I know love, I know,' Ted sighed, 'and I don't suppose we shall ever find out what really happened. Maybe when Lucy comes round she might remember, but I think people often don't after an accident like that.'

Mary put her glass down and grabbed his hand. 'She will come round Ted, won't she?' she cried, tears of shock and exhaustion filling her eyes.

'We've got to believe so Mary, we've got to keep up hope,' and he got up and put his arms round his wife.

'Come on, I'm all in and so are you. We'll go to bed now. We must keep strong for the kids, and don't forget those bloody old cows. There's going to be bellowing in a few hours time if I'm not there,' and he smiled and gently pinched her chin.

They climbed the narrow, creaky old stairs, undressed and fell exhausted into bed. The hot whisky had done its job and neither of them felt like bothering with the normal bed-time ritual of teeth cleaning and washing.

They lay close together, tipped into the middle of the bed by the softness of the old mattress which had seen better days, Ted lying on his side to lessen the chance of him snoring. Mary could tell from his breathing that he had fallen instantly asleep and she envied him his oblivion.

Her mind refused to obey her body and allow her to sleep too, as her thoughts went on whirling round her brain.

How fragile life is when this time last night we were a normal happy family, asleep in our beds with no knowledge of what the future might hold. You read horrid things in the papers but that's other people, not us. She turned restlessly, unable to get comfortable, desperate for the night to pass.

Finally she forced herself to lie still, breathing slowly and deeply as she recited in her mind the lulling words of Keats's poem *To Sleep*. It worked, as it always did for Mary, and at last the hushed casket of her soul was sealed and she fell asleep.

*

It was bumpy and uncomfortable in the back of the van and the students who had come on the day's *sabbing* expedition were relieved to reach the smooth surface of the main road.

The driver was an older man who seldom spoke. He was a member of the Animal Liberation Front and a hard-line activist whose job was to recruit and organise the university students who chose disruption as their preferred way of furthering the cause of animal welfare. In his opinion they lacked commitment and viewed the outing as a lark as much as anything else. He despised them, knowing that when they had achieved a degree in heaven knows what useless subject, most of them would revert to their middle-class personas and run home to *Mummy* and *Daddy*.

The girl sitting beside him was different. Her hatred of the establishment was almost frightening in its intensity. He wondered why she was like she was, as she was a well-spoken, educated sort of girl who he was sure had never suffered any hardship in her life.

He glanced at her out of the corner of his eye as they drew up at a red light *Wouldn't mind giving you one*, he thought, but she had been cool towards him and she didn't look like the *up against a wall* type that suited him. Besides, it was obvious that she and the blond dope in the back, who she called Stevie, were knocking each other off.

Today's lot were new to him and he would be thankful to see the back of them and get on home to a take-away and a pint. He had had a disappointing day himself, for on this occasion the hunt had largely managed to elude its enemies and God alone knew what these idiots had achieved. He hadn't seen anything of them all day until they had all met up again at the van. He didn't care tuppence about the fox but he hated the toffee-nosed scum who pursued it.

He lit a cigarette and focused his attention on the road ahead. Driving conditions were bad with the rain and heavy traffic and he didn't want any trouble with the law. Two of the tyres on the van were borderline and it was the sort of vehicle that the police picked on. The students chattered away to each other but his mind was elsewhere.

'How come you always get the best seat, Gita?'

'How come you don't,' replied the dark girl, flicking back her long, still wet hair.

The others laughed and Sue joined in reluctantly.

'I suppose because I'm one of life's losers and you're one of life's winners.'

'You said it, not me,' intoned Gita in a bored voice.

'Oh come on, Gita,' said Barry, 'you should be in a good mood after a day in the pouring rain saving poor foxy-woxy!'

The others all liked Sue Hanley, who was plump and pretty in an unfashionable sort of way. She was also kind and jolly, but defenceless against Gita's mordant wit.

'Sue's got a point anyway,' said Giles. 'How come you do always manage to avoid the discomfort that we lesser mortals have to endure on our great quest for the salvation of animal-kind?'

'Oh, shut up Giles,' snapped Gita.

The group fell silent for a moment, the atmosphere in the van tense and unfriendly. Everyone was damp and tired and, like the driver, felt that little had been achieved in the way of disruption to the hunt. Still, they should do better next Saturday, for the meet was in a part of the country where it was easier for the saboteurs to keep close to the action.

'You OK Steve?' asked Sue. 'You're very quiet.'

'Six foot two's not the best size for the back of a van,' smiled Steve, 'but otherwise I'm fine thanks.'

'Well you don't look it,' continued Sue, studying his narrow, cadaverous face, 'and I know why, it's that girl isn't it, the girl on the pony, that's what's bothering you.'

'Well yes,' he agreed unwillingly, 'yes it is. I think we should have done something. I don't know what but we shouldn't have just left her lying there.'

'I feel the same way,' said Sue, 'but I don't know what we could have done without risking trouble. I'm sorry though, because stopping cruelty to animals shouldn't involve injury to human beings and for all we know, she might have been dead.'

'All fights against oppression have resulted in loss of

life throughout history,' said Giles. 'Why should ours be any different?'

'Because we would be putting animals on a level with human beings if we embraced that precedent and I don't believe they are,' replied Barry.

'Who says they're not? That's only what you think.' Giles was not prepared to admit defeat too easily.

'Oh come off it mate, your fat Geordie arse is probably squashing the life out of hundreds of innocent creatures at this very minute – you could be the founder member of LAAS – the League Against Arse Squashing! Unless of course you're one of those Jainists, and sweep everything out of the way before you sit down!'

'You've missed the point as usual dickhead,' began Giles, but the others in the back started laughing, so he gave up and joined in, breaking the tension that had built up.

'D'you think we could find out if that girl's OK Steve?' asked Sue.

'I suppose we could though I don't quite know how. If she's bad, it'd probably be reported in their local paper which shouldn't be too difficult to get hold of.'

'What are you lot on about?' The driver suddenly spoke. 'Who is this girl and what happened?'

'Just some stuck-up kid on a pony we came across on the way back,' said Gita. 'She'd obviously been out with the hunt and I shoved a placard at her. The pony jumped and slipped over on the road – that's all.'

'It's not quite all,' cut in Steve, 'she hit her head on the edge of a drain and was unconscious.'

'Steve wanted to get help but I said we should leave well alone,' continued Gita.

Steve had a different recollection of exactly what Gita had said at the time, but he kept quiet, as he had done when the accident happened. That was his trouble, he never could stand up to Gita.

The driver glanced at the blond youth in the mirror; he looked the weak, sensitive type who would have a conscience. She'd obviously got him well and truly by the balls.

'You keep your mouths shut, all of you,' he said. 'We don't want trouble of this sort. Kicking a few horse-faced perverts around is one thing, but attacking kids is bad press.'

'Don't fret yourself, Mr. Big,' sneered Gita, 'we're none of us that stupid.'

She had expected commendation for her actions, not censure, and the driver's tone annoyed her.

'OK,' he said, 'we'll leave it at that.'

The van drew up near the precinct of the University and the five students got out, relieved to be back. Steve and Gita lived together in the same house where Sue had her room, but Barry and Giles went their separate ways as the van drove off.

'Night all,' shouted Barry as he jogged away through the rain.

'You coming to the pub later?' Giles asked the others.

'Don't know,' replied Steve.

'Depends on what her ladyship has in store for you I suppose!' joked Giles. 'See you later if you do,' and he set off for his digs, anxious to get out of his wet clothes that were now cold and clammy.

Sue had already opened the front door of the solid, red brick Victorian house where they lodged, and as they parted in the hall, she asked, 'Would you two like to share some lasagne later on? There's plenty for three and you're welcome if you want.'

Steve turned to Gita for her answer and to his surprise, she accepted.

'We'll bring some booze and see you a bit later,' he said.

Sue was a good cook, much better than Gita, whose

talents lay in a different direction and Steve was hungry after his day in the open air. He also felt relief that Gita's black mood seemed to have passed and that he would not have to spend money he had not got taking her out for a meal. Besides, he was happy to stay in, as he liked the house with its spacious rooms and high, plaster-moulded ceilings, so different from his home near Southampton.

The students who lived in the house were lucky, because the landlord, who owned four of the terraced houses in the street, liked to keep his properties in good condition. Neither did he view his student lodgers as tenants to be exploited for high rents with minimal maintenance.

They were all in their last year of their various degree courses and Sue and Gita had rented their rooms for nearly two years. Steve had moved in with Gita shortly after they first met six months ago, and to Gita it was home.

She had severed all contact with her parents some time ago, and made it clear that she had no desire to see them. The distraught mother had turned up on the doorstep early one summer evening, when Sue had answered the bell. She had smiled at the dark haired, anxious looking woman who stood there, and had noted the expensive, casual elegance of the woman's clothes and her well-cut hair. Sue wondered who on earth she could be.

'I'm Diana Taverner, Gita's mother,' she had said. 'Is she in by any chance?'

Gita had been in and there had been a terrible scene. Mrs Taverner had left in tears, leaving Sue shocked by some of the things she had overheard Gita shouting at her mother. Shortly after, Gita had received a letter from her father informing her that he had stopped her allowance and that henceforth, she was on her own. Gita seemed undismayed and had shrugged her shoulders, saying that she had not wanted his *dirty capitalist money* in the first place.

As Sue lay soaking in her bath she thought about Gita, as she had many times before. She was a strange person, difficult to reach a conclusion about and pigeon-hole. Sue liked to be able to pigeon-hole people, in the same way that she liked to keep her room neat and well-organised.

Gita never spoke about her home, family or childhood, and as she had no close friends, it was impossible to find out. Steve was so different, both in terms of background and personality, and Sue found it hard to understand their relationship. *Sex I suppose*, she thought wistfully, but a loud banging on the shared bathroom door broke into her thoughts.

'You gone down the plug-hole or something?' a voice shouted. 'Sorry Sophie, won't be a minute,' she called back, recognising the voice of a girl whom she rather disliked. Needless to say Gita had managed to get the only room in the house that had its own bathroom, and Sue wondered how she could afford it without the support of her parents.

She pulled the plug and got out, taking care not to slosh water all over the tiled floor. As the last of her bath water gurgled away, she swished the grimy bits down the plug, donned her utilitarian bathrobe and slippers and headed back to her room.

On the floor above, Gita peeled off her wet clothes, dropping them in a heap where she stood in her shirt and brief, black lace pants. She never wore a bra and as she walked towards Steve, she started slowly to undo the buttons of her shirt.

'Come on Stevie,' she smiled, putting her arms round him and pushing her lower body into his, 'you know what I want.' She fastened her mouth onto his before he could answer.

Steve felt tired and ill at ease with himself. He had hoped Gita's inevitable demands would have come later, when they were in bed and he had had time to relax, satisfy his hunger and have a drink. But he could never resist her slim, craving body, and as she ripped his clothes off the blood rushed into his cock and they collapsed on the floor where they stood.

'God you're good Stevie,' she smiled afterwards, victorious satisfaction gleaming out of her rapacious eyes. 'Come on, let's go and eat Miss Goody Two-shoes bourgeois lasagne. Bring plenty of wine, I feel like a long night.'

'You're not bad yourself,' he smiled back as he went to fetch the wine. Sex with Gita was always ferocious and quick, and it reminded Steve of his mother's pressure cooker which had fascinated him as a child. He sometimes wished she could be more like a casserole – long, slow and tender.

Sue's door was open and supper nearly ready when they arrived. 'Hi, won't be a minute. Will you do the wine Steve, the glasses are on the table.' She knew instinctively what they had been up to by the conquering glitter in Gita's sly green eyes; eyes that said *poor plain little Sue – can't get herself a screw,* but Sue was only too thankful to have Gita's acid mood replaced by one of scornful condescension if it meant that they could all enjoy a companionable evening together.

Lasagne, green salad and garlic bread arrived on the table. Grapes and a ripe-smelling camembert waited on the side.

'Help yourself Steve, there's plenty and I don't want any left over.'

'Got any ketchup?'

'Hang on, I'll get it.'

'Disgusting stuff Steven Tanner,' gibed Gita, 'shows up your dubious origins!'

'Terrible, isn't it!' agreed Steve, liberally squirting ketchup all over his food. 'That's what happens when you come from a council house near Southampton.'

'Hmm – this is delicious,' he raised his glass to Sue.

'Didn't you have ketchup at home then Gita?' asked Sue.

'Good God no, my beloved oh so middle-class parents would rather die than allow a bottle in the house. Supposing the char woman had told the neighbours!'

'Well, at least you've got some parents – I can't think why you hate them so much.' replied Sue, wondering if two glasses of wine had completely turned her head that she should be so bold with Gita.

'Of course I've got parents – everyone has you know. Don't tell me you still think babies are brought by the stork!' Gita burst out laughing as she refilled her glass.

'Actually Gita, I was adopted. Not knowing your biological parents is almost the same as not having any, and although I love Mum and Dad, I still can't help wondering sometimes who I really am.'

'Did you ever try and find out?' asked Steve.

'When I was sixteen, I tried to find out who my real mother was. I didn't care much about my father, but I desperately wanted to know how a woman could give her baby away and why.'

'Perhaps she was dead or something,' said Gita. 'She might have died having you, or maybe when you popped out and she first saw you she died of fright!'

'Gita!' said Steve sharply.

'Sorry Sue, but honestly, this parent-child thing is grossly overrated in my opinion. Anyway, go on about your search for your mother.'

'I never found out in the end. You see, it upset my parents that I wanted to know and I thought well, what does it matter really when they have given me so much love and happiness, so I let it go and now I seldom think about it.'

There was a brief silence, broken by Steve.

'Would you like to have children of your own, Sue?'

'Oh yes! At least two and preferably four.'

'Yuck, how horrible,' commented Gita, 'all that shitting and puking and silly baby talk – not to mention your ruined figure – no thanks.'

'D'you think your mother thought that about you then Gita?' asked Steve.

'She didn't have to, did she. She employed a nanny till I was ten, then she sent me to boarding school – about the only sensible thing she ever did in her life.'

'Gosh, they must be rich,' said Sue naively. 'More cheese?'

Gita pushed away the proffered cheese before answering.

'Nobody should have so much more money than others, but worst of all is my parents' obsession with appearances. Everything has to fit in with their vision of the upper middle classes, and that includes their daughter. I hate their hypocrisy and all that they stand for – and if you really want to know, I hate them,' she finished.

'At least wealthy people like them help to keep the nation's coffers full so that people like me can get educated,' said Steve. 'Think how much money income and inheritance taxes produce – and I bet you wouldn't have enjoyed being raised poor.'

'Don't be such a bore.'

'And why do you go sabbing – is it all part of your anti-establishment principles or are you really concerned about animal welfare?'

'Go and get another bottle Stevie darling, and then I might tell you.'

'No more for me thanks,' said Sue. 'I'll make some coffee.'

Steve was back in a minute and pulled the cork from the wine before filling his own glass and putting the bottle down in front of Gita.

'Well,' he said, 'there's the wine, now let's have your answer.'

'My answer is that I couldn't give a damn about foxes, but I hate those bloody superior bastards who go hunting. They are all part of the great British class structure that needs annihilating.'

'Honestly Gita, you do talk rot sometimes,' said Sue bravely. 'There's lots of working class people who go out with the hunt as well as nobs, even I know that and the days of the fat, red-faced squire riding rough-shod over the peasants have long gone.'

'Is that so Miss Know-It-All. Well shall I tell you something, the best thing that happened to me all day was frightening that pony.'

'Oh Gita, you can't *really* mean that,' cried Sue.

'Of course she doesn't,' put in Steve quickly. 'Come on Gita, you're pissed, have some coffee and let's go to bed. I'm whacked and I've got a lot of work to do tomorrow for an essay.'

'How dare you answer for me,' spat Gita, 'I meant what I said and if you two want to get all sobby about some bloody kid, you carry on.' She slammed her near-empty glass down on the table, the thin stem snapping on impact. She marched out of the room, leaving the spilled red wine to spread over the table cloth like the blood from Lucy's head on the road.

'Oh Steve, I'm so sorry. That was all my fault, I should never have answered her back and I'd so hoped we could all have had a nice evening together.'

'Don't be silly Sue, of course it wasn't your fault. You know what Gita's like when she's had a few too many – forget it – if she wants to go off in a huff that's her lookout but I'm sorry about your glass.'

'That doesn't matter, they were only cheap ones – you'd better go though Steve.'

'No, I think for once she can get on with it. Let's finish

our coffee then I'll give you a hand with the washing up. With any luck she might be asleep by then.' and he smiled at Sue's anxious face.

'I want to talk to you anyway. I know you feel the same way as I do about that girl today, and I thought I'd tell you that I've decided to try and find out if she was OK. It's been bothering me you know. My sister's not much older, and I wouldn't like to think of what it would do to our family if anything awful happened to her.'

'I'm glad you think that way and you're right, I do too, but I don't see what we can do without incriminating ourselves. I mean, the police don't seem to care much about most of what we do, but this could be different.'

'I know, and I've thought about it. There's nothing much we can do, but I'd just like to *know*.'

'I wonder sometimes whether we're doing the right thing by going sabbing. I don't know anything much about hunting or life in the countryside, or the people who live there, do you? It does seem one of those issues where emotion overrides fact.'

'You may have a point but you can't get away from the fact that it must be wrong to chase and kill an animal for pleasure. After all, most MPs want hunting banned and they're supposed to be the voice of the people. I can't go next Saturday anyway, it's my mum's birthday, and I want to go home and see her. I might do a bit of sleuthing on Sunday though. I know Mum and Dad are having lunch with Nan and Auntie Jean so it would be a good opportunity.'

'Aaah!' yawned Sue, stretching her arms above her head. 'I'm sleepy, don't bother about the washing up, I'll do it in the morning – I'm for bed.'

'Suits me and thanks for supper, it was great. See yer.'

'Night Steve.'

To Steve's relief, Gita was asleep when he came in. As he slipped quietly into bed beside her, he realised that it was the first time in their relationship that he would have been unable to satisfy her demands. He lay still, hoping that she would not wake up.

*

Mary sighed, and pushed a stray lock of hair back off her forehead as she stood at the kitchen sink, peeling potatoes.

Ted had insisted that she invite Sally and Derek over for supper. Ben had gone out to a McDonalds and cinema evening with a school friend and he thought some company would be good for her.

He was right of course, but just now she felt no desire to see anyone or do anything. In fact, Mary did not know what she felt like. Since the initial shock of Lucy's accident, a dull weight had settled on her and all her normal energy and motivation seemed to have vanished. She struggled through her essential, everyday tasks but it was only when she sat by her still unconscious daughter's bedside that any life returned to her.

Mary spent as much time as she was able at the hospital, where she found a strange peace in the quiet cocoon of Lucy's little room in the Intensive Care Unit. The rhythmic swish of the artificial ventilator somehow reassured her and she liked the warm, clean atmosphere, brightened by cards from family and friends.

Mary always held her daughter's hand. She would shut her eyes and will, with all her inner strength, that her life force would somehow flow into the unconscious girl and bring her back.

Never for one moment did she give up hope, but when the time came to leave the hospital, and walk out of the main doors across the tarmac to the car park, the weight would crush down on her again and a wrenching panic would grip her. She felt like an alien being, who had stepped out of her cosmos into a world of disorder and fear.

Today's visit had been no different and as she got up to go home, she explained to Lucy why she was leaving earlier than usual. 'Dad wanted Mr and Mrs Vicary over to supper so I must go and do some cooking. Ben's staying with Freddie Williams, they are going to the cinema, then to McDonalds for a *blow out* as your brother calls it. Goodbye darling and I'll see you tomorrow.'

At first Mary had felt a fool, talking to an unconscious person, but the consultant encouraged her. 'Why not Mrs. Cardew,' he said, 'anything that might help reach Lucy is worth doing and if it helps you too, then carry on.'

She liked the man, who was kind but unsentimental, and after their talk, Mary had no inhibitions about chatting away to Lucy as if she were still a normal, responsive child. The doctor had guessed right, it did help her too.

The potatoes were sizzling in the oven, nestling round a sirloin of beef, and Mary had nearly finished cutting up the cabbage when Ted came in from milking.

'Hello love,' he kissed her, 'that smells good, I can't wait. I'd better hurry and clean up, Sally and Derek'll be here in a minute.'

'Ted, there's no change.'

'I know that Mary. I know if there had been it would have been the first thing you'd said,' and he put his big, calloused hand on her shoulder for a moment before turning away to go upstairs and change. He knew his wife wanted more from him than he could give, but each man had to deal with anguish in his own way.

Ted's guts churned every time he thought about his daughter, still and silent in that hospital bed. Even the sight of the pony distressed him. He had wanted to get rid of it, but Mary had been shocked.

'Sell Pickles? *Never, never, never!*' she had cried, 'Lucy would never forgive us,' and that had been the end of it. He had to cope in his own way, and his way was the way of his kind. The land gave life and the land took it away, but the wheel kept turning and there was little they could do to change it.

He did worry though, about Mary's apparent refusal to acknowledge that Lucy might never regain consciousness. That one day, the unthinkable decision might have to be made and the machines turned off.

He heard the back door bang, then voices floated up to him from below. Dragging a clean sweater over his head, he went downstairs to greet his guests.

'Hello Ted dear,' Sally jumped up and kissed him warmly. 'How are the old cows, milking properly?'

Ted laughed as he returned her kiss. Sally, early mornings and slurry did not go together, and her customary enquiry never required an answer.

'Sorry I wasn't down to greet you, you can blame the old cows! Have you both got a drink?'

'Yes thanks, Mary's looked after us in your absence. I was just saying Derek, wasn't I, that Mrs Gable at the Newsagents – the greatest gossip of all time – reported that a strange young man came in on Sunday, asking whether anyone round here had been injured in a riding accident recently.'

Mary came back into the sitting room and picked up her glass of cider. 'Supper's ready, let's go and eat, but I want to hear about this Sal, it all sounds a bit odd.'

'Great! I'm starving and I need my weekly dose of BSE – come on you men – stop banging on about the plight of the farmer.'

When they were all settled round the kitchen table, Sally continued with her interrupted news. 'Yes, can you believe it, old Ma Gable told Poppy when she went in for some awful teenage magazine she buys – I don't approve at all, it's full of ridiculous diets and tips on how to get your man and....'

'But *what* did Ma Gable say, what was the man like?'

broke in Mary, knowing how her friend could lose the thread of her stories and go rambling off at a tangent.

'Well, according to Poppy, she said he was a young bloke, casually dressed but nicely mannered, and what Ma G called *sort of respectable like* whatever that might mean!'

'Probably means he didn't hold her up at knife point and demand her virtue and the contents of the till!'

'Really Derek, what ridiculous things you say sometimes. Let me finish my story. Apparently he claimed to be doing market research for a company that manufactures riding equipment, and they're trying to plug the safety angle for their latest range.'

'Sounds a bit phoney to me,' said Mary. 'Anyway, does history relate how our worthy gossip replied?'

Sally laughed. 'You know what the old bat's like – according to Poppy she said *and what if I do, it's no business of yours young man and people who go poking their noses round other peoples' corners get them bitten off!* Then he bought a packet of wine gums and left.'

'She does come up with the most extraordinary expressions, but it's all rather strange I think,' mused Mary.

'Oh, I don't know,' replied Derek between mouthfuls, 'why shouldn't he be genuine? After all, this is a horsey area and market research is all the rage nowadays. Just coincidence I reckon.'

'I don't believe in coincidences.'

'Well I agree with Derek, love. Pass the mustard would you, and help yourself to more Derek if you want. Anyway, what other explanation could there be?'

'I don't know Ted, but maybe this man knows something about the accident. Maybe he was involved in some way but doesn't want anybody to know.'

'I must say Mary,' chipped in Sally, 'for once I agree with the men. I think you should take it at face value and forget the whole thing. Derek, you are *such* a pig, no wonder your clothes are getting tight!' Sally watched as her husband heaped more food onto his plate, before chattering on.

'Have you heard about Eve Stalbridge being sacked from the Supporters Club Committee. Apparently she told Fiona Barrington that Martin was a nasty little lecher and he'd tried to put his hand up her skirt at the Whist Drive – what a scream!'

'Poor old Martin, he must be getting short-sighted,' said Derek, 'if I'd had my hand up Eve's skirt it would probably have gangrene by now!' And they all laughed, breaking the tension that had begun to creep into the evening.

The Vicarys left soon after 10 when Ted went up to bed while Mary finished the washing up. She had to admit that Ted had been right, the evening had done her good and helped take her out of herself, for a short time at least.

She went up to bed, feeling that tonight, sleep might come a little easier than it had done since Lucy's accident. As she drifted off, Sally's story about the strange young man came back to her and her dreams were troubled by a faceless presence hanging over Lucy's bed.

*

'Come in, the door's open,' called out Sue when she heard the knock. She was struggling with an essay and was delighted for an excuse to stop, and even more pleased when Steve turned out to be the instrument of interruption.

'Sorry to barge in, I didn't think you'd be working.'

'Neither did I till I realised how behind I'm getting. You know Steve, I'm not sure I'm cut out for the academic life. I know I'll only get a bum degree and where will that get me. All I really want is a nice little house, a nice large man and a brood of kids!'

'Don't let Gita hear you say that,' laughed Steve, 'she

wouldn't approve at all!'

'Like a coffee? How is she by the way, I haven't seen her around for a bit.'

'No, she's been in London for a few days. All very mysterious. Actually we haven't been getting on too well recently.'

'Oh Steve, I'm sorry to hear that – poor old you.'

'Yes well, I suppose we're not the first couple to have a row! I don't really know what to do about it yet, but I guess when Gita gets back from London things'll sort themselves out. But that's not what I came to talk to you about. I've found out about the girl on the pony.'

'Good heavens Steve, tell all. However did you track her down? I can't wait to hear.'

'I went to the nearest village to where we were when we saw her and pretended I was doing market research for a riding equipment manufacturer. Being Sunday everywhere was shut except the newsagent, so I went in but the old harridan wouldn't play. In fact she virtually told me to get lost, but the landlord of the local pub was quite happy to talk.' Steve paused for a mouthful of coffee.

'Come on Steve, don't keep me in suspense.'

Steve put down the mug and frowned as he continued.

'It's not very good news I fear. She's in a coma in Barstock Hospital.'

'Oh no, how awful – what have we done?'

'We've ruined somebody's life, that's what, and probably her family's too. If she dies, you could call it murder.' They looked at each other in silence as the implications of Steve's words sunk in.

'Look Sue, I've got to dash but let's go to the Whistling Parrot this evening. I'll stand you a dish of the day and then we can talk properly.'

'OK. I'll be ready about 7.30 so we can get in before it gets too crowded.'

The door banged shut behind Steve and Sue was left alone to think about the news he had brought. The essay was abandoned, and brewing herself another mug of coffee, she sat down and tried to bring order to her muddled thoughts.

She had to admit that the thought of going out with Steve was exciting, as her feelings for him ran much deeper than just friendship. But the reason for the pub visit distressed her. She was horrified by what had happened, but what could they do. And there was Gita. After all, it had been Gita who had caused the accident in the first place.

*

'You look good tonight,' said Steve, as they sat down to a plate of sausage and mash.

'Must be the dim lighting,' laughed Sue, blushing awkwardly.

'Don't be silly, false modesty never became anyone and you're not some simpering Austen heroine.' But Steve was surprised that the compliment had rolled so spontaneously off his tongue. How could you compare steady old Sue to the beautiful, alluring Gita. Yet somehow her honest, homely face brought with it a sense of ease that he found comforting and good. What a pity that the one quality seldom went with the other.

He wondered briefly if women assessed men in the same way and if so, how did Sue rate him. He wondered also, what she would be like in bed, but his instinct told him that it would not be easy to find out. She was not the type that slept around, and he had never been aware of her having a relationship.

'Don't be conned by all that maidenly simpering – beneath our heroines' chaste muslin gowns, lustful passions stir!' They laughed together for a moment, forkfuls of sausage poised between plate and mouth.

'Seriously though Steve, I feel so bad about that poor

girl, tell me all you found out about her.'

Steve refilled their glasses, his face pensive as he watched the thin, slightly purple wine flow from the bottle. He put it down on the table and sat back in his chair, food for the moment forgotten.

'Her name's Lucy Cardew. She's 13 or thereabouts, and has a younger brother called Ben. Her parents are ordinary, decent people who seem well-liked in the village and work hard to make a living farming. Mr Cardew's a tenant and so was his father and Mrs Cardew's a local woman from a similar background. It seems things are pretty difficult at the moment for farmers and these people are certainly not rich or upper class.'

As Steve paused for a drink, Sue leaned forward over the cluttered little table, her eyes full of anguish.

'I wish you hadn't found out her name and about the family, it somehow makes it all much worse. I can see them now as real people with feelings like mine and I don't like it.'

'Well, we wanted to find out, and now we have. Like I said, the landlord was a talkative sort of fellow, particularly as I had a pint or two of the local brew. Apparently everyone likes the kid and is pretty devastated by what happened. I played the commiserating stranger, you know the sort of thing – *how awful, does anyone know what happened?* and the answer is they don't. It seems she was a good rider and a sensible sort of girl.'

'But how bad is she Steve, did the man know?'

'No. He just said she was in intensive care in a coma. He didn't know any details. But guess what happened next.'

'What?'

'Some old bloke comes in and leans on the bar, obviously a regular because the landlord called him Alfie, and asked if he wanted his *usual,* then pulled a pint. Then he told this Alfie character about me and what I was doing – typical pub gossip – and our talk about the girl. Old Alfie slurps his beer and of course, has his say. He knew sabs'd been out that day and his view was that we'd caused the accident.'

Sue gasped, 'Oh Steve, how *awful*. Whatever did you say?'

'Well, nothing of course – he's got no evidence and anyway, I reckon he's just an old windbag who no one would listen to. He and the barman went on talking about the rights and wrongs of it all, you know, the usual stuff, so I downed my pint, said I'd got to be getting on and left.'

'What an extraordinary thing for this Alfie person to say, he can't possibly have any proof can he?'

'No, of course not but let's face it, he's right isn't he. But don't worry Sue, he was just guessing and by chance, happened to hit the nail on the head. Not a thing he does very often by the look of him!'

'I'm sorry to keep on about it, but I do feel dreadful about what happened. Imagine if it was your sister Debs in that hospital, and your mum sitting there praying she would come back to life. I think I shall feel guilty forever.'

'You don't need to feel guilty at all. Apart from being there, you had nothing to do with it. It was Gita who frightened the pony and me who was so feeble about getting help.'

The two students sat in silence, the noisy chatter and clatter of the busy eating-house swelling around them as they finished their now cold food. Sue was the first to break the silence.

'Shall I tell you what I would like to do? I know it sounds a bit weird and pointless, but I would like to take some flowers to the hospital for Lucy. We could just leave them in reception with her name on and nobody could possibly trace us.'

'I suppose it'd be all right as long as we're careful – and

I don't think it's weird. It's a nice thought, though I can't see that it makes anything better. Come on, I'll go and pay then let's go back and have some of your best coffee, I've nearly had today.'

They climbed the stairs in silence, and as they arrived at the door of Sue's room, Steve said 'I'll just go on up and turn the fire on, the bedroom's freezing. Won't be a minute so get that coffee machine rolling.'

Sue stifled a pang of disappointment that Steve had not even contemplated trying to spend the night with her. Whether or not she would have let him was beside the point.

Don't be silly, she told herself, *he's in love with Gita and you wouldn't think much of him if he tried to sleep with you.*

Sue would rather die than admit it to her friends, but she had only ever had sex with a man once. Her initiation had been an unpleasant affair when, after a first year party, she had got rather drunk and allowed her virginity to be claimed by some clueless youth who had grunted and heaved briefly, called her by the wrong name, and disappeared before breakfast the next morning.

His name was Andrew, and she had never seen him again.

She was left feeling dirty and hung-over and wondered, as she showered away his smell the next morning, why it was that everyone raved about sex.

The coffee was belching in her old-fashioned percolator when Steve rushed into the room.

'Sorry Sue, Gita's back. She never tells me what she's doing but she's here and well...' he paused, 'you know, she won't be too pleased if I stop for coffee and we can't talk about Lucy in front of her.'

Sue's heart sank, and she felt an unaccustomed stab of resentment.

'Never mind, I didn't want a late night anyway. And,'

she added as an afterthought, 'I'm pleased for you that she's back. Thanks for taking me out and see you tomorrow.'

The door banged shut and Sue was left with her unwanted coffee.

*

'So, while the cat's away, little Stevie goes out to play.'

Steve looked at his lover as her words greeted him on his return to her room. She reminded him of a cat, with her sleek black hair, green eyes and feline body. Her claws too were retractable, but very sharp.

'Hardly playing, Gita. Sue and I went to the Parrot for a meal, that's all. I can't be expected to starve just because you disappear to London and don't tell me when you're coming back. What have you been up to anyway?'

'What I have been *up to* as you put it, is entirely my own business.' Then she smiled, and winding her arms round his neck, nibbled his ear.

'Hmm, if it's only Miss Goody Two-shoes, I don't think I've too much to worry about, do you? I can't imagine that her sexual charms would prove much of a threat.' But sensing Steve's lack of response, she dropped her arms and laughing, turned away to pour herself a drink.

'Gita, I wish you wouldn't talk like that. As you perfectly well know, Sue's just a friend who happens to live in the same house. I like her and we had something we wanted to discuss – to do with work,' he added quickly.

'God how boring, but then I suppose you upwardly mobile state school types take their degrees terribly seriously.'

'For heaven's sake shut up. I've missed you and couldn't wait for you to come back, but you've hardly given me the same impression.'

Steve followed Gita and poured himself a lager, astonished that he had told her to shut up. He had never asserted himself in their relationship, having always been the one who gave way. He expected a volley of verbal abuse, but to his surprise, Gita sat down and calmly lit a cigarette, watching him through the smoke that she blew out of her pursed, dog's-bottom mouth.

'The only person ever to tell me to shut up was my father. I told him then that I would never speak to him again and I never have.'

'You will Gita, when the time comes and you want *daddy's* money. It's easy for people like you to play at being anti-capitalists, because you know that at the end of the day blood'll be thicker than water. Your degree doesn't matter a damn to you, but to people like me and Sue, people who you seem to despise, it matters a great deal. And doing well is a small way of repaying our parents for all the sacrifices they made to help get us here.'

'God, you sanctimonious prig – take your bloody junk and fuck off out of my room – *now*!' she screamed, 'before I throw it out.'

'Fine by me – I've had enough of your bitchiness anyway.'

*

Steve sat in Sue's room, drinking the re-heated coffee. It was after midnight by the time he arrived, seeking sanctuary at her door. His possessions were piled in an untidy heap on the landing and he felt blitzed, yet at the same time, strangely relieved.

'It was going to happen sooner or later,' he said, 'but I never thought it would be quite like this. It's the first time I've ever had the guts to stand up to her.'

'Poor old you, Steve. I'm so sorry, I really am.'

Sue thought how typically feeble her words of condolence sounded. All she ever seemed to say was *I'm so sorry*, but she could never think of anything better. Truthfully, on this occasion she was not sorry at all. Gita unnerved her, and the prospect of being able to see Steve without her being there to make Sue feel a clumsy, sexless, idiot was one to savour.

'Look Sue, thanks for rescuing me. It won't take me long to sort something out, but if I could camp down on your sofa till then it'd be great. We'll go away this weekend if you like, and take your flowers to the hospital.'

'Oh yes!' enthused Sue, 'I really would like to do that and maybe we could find a cheap B&B and spend Saturday night away from here – let the dust settle a bit.'

'Why not?' Steve yawned, 'but for now I just want to crash out and forget the whole thing.'

*

'Can I come to the hospital with you this afternoon Mum? Football's off as it's too wet and Freddie's going with his mum to visit some boring old lady.'

'Of course you can Ben, provided Dad doesn't want any help. Have you asked him?'

'Yep and he said OK.'

'Lovely, let's go then. It will be nice for me to have some company. We won't stay too long so you can give him a hand when we get back. He's working terribly hard at the moment and this never-ending rain isn't helping.'

'I know, and he said if we can't get the cows out early this year the silage'll run out and with the cost of cake and the price of milk we shall be broke.'

Mary smiled at her son's repetition of Ted's mutterings, and at the serious expression on his face.

'Don't worry Ben, if that happens you can always go and get a job as a football coach!'

'Don't be silly Mum.'

Light-hearted moments were things to be treasured nowadays, and Mary was glad that Ben wanted to come with her to see his sister. It would mean curtailing her visit, as she knew he would soon get bored of sitting by a silent Lucy, but on this occasion, she would not mind.

Ben chattered away inconsequentially as they sped along the road to the hospital and, when they arrived, he ran on ahead to be first into Lucy's room. As Mary joined him, she heard him greeting his sister before they sat down together beside the bed.

After a little while, as Mary had anticipated, he began to fidget.

'Can I go now Mum and wait for you in the car? I've bought my book and I don't think Lucy looks like waking up today. Wish she'd hurry up though.'

'Of course you can. I won't be long but don't go wandering round the hospital will you, go straight back to the car.'

'OK. See you later, bye.'

Mary sighed as he closed the door. The boy appeared remarkably undismayed by what had happened, and it never seemed to enter his head that Lucy might not recover. Perhaps it was his way of blocking out something he was unable to come to terms with, or perhaps it was the thoughtless optimism of youth. She hoped very much it was the latter.

'Hello Mrs Cardew, did I see young Ben disappearing off down the passage?'

Mary turned to smile at the cheerful young nurse, who came in carrying a vase of flowers.

'Hello Rose, yes you did. He wanted to come but as you can imagine, sitting still for more than about five minutes is not his idea of fun!'

'Ah well, that's only normal for a lad of his age. What about a cuppa? I expect you could do with one.'

'Oh Rose, that's sweet of you but I promised Ben I wouldn't be long and Ted could use a hand at evening milking. Those are nice flowers, did another patient have too many and think of Lucy? How kind.'

'No,' answered the nurse in surprise. 'They came through from reception a few minutes ago. Rita just said they were for Lucy Cardew.'

'Was there a card with them?' inquired Mary.

'Not that I know of, but ask Mrs Edwards on your way out. Maybe they left a message or the card fell off or something.'

'Yes, that's a good idea – I will. Odd though, I can't think who would have sent them. Anyway, I had better go or Ben will be playing Michael Schumacher round the car park!'

The nurse smiled at Mary's little joke. 'See you tomorrow then Mrs Cardew, and take care.'

Poor woman, she thought, as she watched her hurrying away down the long, drab passage, *how long would it be before she might have to face the fact that her daughter may never recover.*

Mrs Edwards knew little more than the nurse about the mysterious flowers. An ordinary, pleasant looking young couple, who didn't give a name and seemed anxious to be gone. That was all she had to say.

Mary ran through the rain and jumped in beside Ben, who seemed quite happy reading his book.

'Funny thing Ben,' she said as she started the car, 'some people left a lovely bunch of flowers for Lucy, but no name or card. Who on earth could they be I wonder?'

'Come on man – kill 'im,' shouted Ben, completely ignoring his mother.

'*Please* put that book down and listen to what I say.'

'I did listen Mum!' exclaimed Ben in his best hard-done by voice. 'I saw them but what's such a big deal about flowers.'

'Oh Ben, sometimes I could throttle you – that's just the sort of thing your father would say. Did you recognise them? Perhaps they were from the school, I'll ring up Mrs Summers when we get home.'

'Don't think so, I've never seen them before and I'm pretty good at faces. I got their car number though. I was being Sherlock Holmes and it was a crummy old car painted horrible colours so I noticed it.'

'Keep that number will you, I want to know who they were and why they brought flowers for Lucy.'

'OK. I'll put it in your bag now, I don't want it anymore. What's for tea?'

'Your favourite thing, wait and see with guess what sauce.'

Ben gave his mother a withering look, wishing she wouldn't treat him like a baby. What a difficult business growing up could be. He settled back in his seat, his thoughts turning to his plans for the forthcoming evening as the car sped on through the half-light of the wet winter afternoon.

*

It was Monday morning and Mary was in the local sub-station, trying her best to persuade PC Watkins to trace the owner of the mysterious car.

'You do realise we are not supposed to give out this sort of information Mrs Cardew, don't you?'

'Oh I know Tom but please, you do see it's only because I want to be able to thank them and find out how they know Lucy. You must understand how I feel and I'm sure you and Joy would be just the same if it was Linda in hospital.'

She tried to stop a note of irritation from creeping into her voice, for slow old Tom was far more likely to respond to cajolery than bluster.

'Look ye here Mrs C, seeing as how your young lass's in trouble and just between the two of us, I'll see what I can do. After all, I shan't be here much longer, and I don't suppose it's such a crime as to affect my pension!'

'Tom – you're a wonder! You know how sorry we all are about the sub-station closing down and losing you. How long will it take to find out?'

'You got any shopping to do?'

'Tons unfortunately.'

'Well you call back on your way home and we'll see what's what.'

'Thank you Tom, I really do appreciate your help – see you in a bit.'

Mary had to stop herself from rushing flat out through the Monday morning shop, so great was her anxiety to get back to Tom and discover the identity of the anonymous flower donors.

There was a lot to do, as they always tried to save fuel by limiting shopping trips to the bare minimum, so it was some time before she was finished. The other problem now was bumping into friends and acquaintances who sought news of Lucy. Mary appreciated their kindly enquiries, but wished she did not have to see them and say again and again that there was no change.

Her heart was beating rapidly as she drew up outside the police house, but Tom smiled as she came in and, with a wink and a nudge, handed her a discreetly folded piece of paper.

'Now you remember what I said – between you and me.'

'Oh, I will Tom, I will. Don't worry and thanks a million – love to Joy and see you soon.'

She hurried back to the car and once in the driving seat, sat back and stared at the piece of paper. Mary knew intuitively that the information contained therein would solve the riddle of her daughter's accident. She took a deep breath and unfolded the paper:

Steven John Tanner, 26 Linden Way, Hedge End, Southampton

'Now I shall find you,' she whispered, 'and you can tell me what happened to my Lucy.'

At last the house was empty, with Ted out feeding the ewes and Ben at school. Mary had decided not to say anything about her plan to track down the unidentified couple, as she felt that Ted would try to dissuade her, and would not agree with her actions.

Directory Enquiries provided the telephone number, and as the disembodied female voice repeated it in her carefully articulated speech, Mary scribbled it down on the back of an old envelope.

She punched out the numbers, tearing at a rough cuticle on her thumb as the rings went unanswered the other end.

'Come on somebody,' she muttered aloud, 'for heaven's sake pick up the phone.'

'Hello, Mrs Tanner speaking.' The voice on the other end was female and pleasant, but not the voice of a young woman.

'Oh hello, I was hoping to speak to Steven, is he at home by any chance?'

'No, he's away at university I'm afraid. Can I help at all, I'm his mother.'

'If you could give me his number that would be most helpful. It's nothing urgent but I need to speak to him about a mail order he placed with us recently and for some reason he gave this number.'

Mary prayed that Mrs Tanner would swallow her spurious story and her prayers were answered. She thanked the woman, wrote down the number and replaced the receiver. Duplicity was alien to Mary's nature and she felt flustered and wretched as she made the call that might answer her question.

'Hello,' an abrupt sounding young male voice answered.

'Oh hello, is Steven Tanner there please?'

'Hang on, he might be.'

She heard the voice shouting, 'Steve, phone.' Then there was a pause and some unidentifiable background noise.

'Steve Tanner here, who's speaking?'

Mary's mouth went dry and she nearly replaced the handset.

'My name is Mary Cardew, I'm Lucy's mother.'

For a brief moment that seemed like an eternity, there was total silence on the other end. Then, 'I'm sorry, I think you must have the wrong number, I don't know anyone called Cardew.'

'Do you drive an old purple and yellow painted car?'

'Yes I do, why?'

'Well, I think you went to Barstock Hospital last Saturday with some flowers for my daughter. I'd like to thank you but I'd also like to know why.'

'Ah yes – well – I don't quite know what to say.'

Put the phone down, screamed a voice in Steve's head, but something inside himself stopped him. He was shocked rigid by the call, and by how she had traced him so quickly. He wanted to buy time. But time was not for sale, and she would haunt him forever if he did not face up to the crisis now. Her nemesis would be his conscience, and then there was Sue. She had a stake in this too, and Steve knew what she would want him to do.

'Look Mrs Cardew, I think we should meet. It's a long story, about the flowers I mean, and much better told face to face.'

'I think that's very necessary, and without delay. I'd like to fix a time and place now.' Mary found it impossible to sound friendly in any way.

They arranged to meet the following Thursday, in a pub that was halfway-house between the two of them. Mary felt quite calm now and as she walked back to the kitchen to make herself a cup of tea, she wished she could go to sleep and wake up on Thursday morning. The two days she would have to wait before confronting this man seemed endless, but time would pass, as it always did, and then she would know the truth.

*

'We're going to be late Steve,' fussed Sue, awash with nerves, 'can't you speed up a bit?'

'Give the old girl a chance, she's nearly as old as you and I can't see you going any faster!'

'Hmm, I fear athletics were never my strong point. Let's hope Mrs Cardew doesn't think we're not coming and goes home.'

'She won't and we're only running about five minutes late so stop panicking.'

'Sorry – but I'm so frightened – I mean what exactly are we going to say.'

'Look Sue, we've been over this several times already. Leave the talking to me and I shall tell the truth, but I am not bringing Gita's name into it at any price – OK?'

Sue nodded and bit her lip. She knew that Steve had not yet come to terms with splitting up from Gita, and although she was sure they would never get back together again, her friendship with Steve remained platonic and showed no sign of developing into the relationship Sue so desperately wanted.

They arrived, as predicted, a bare five minutes late and Mary guessed who they were as soon as they walked through the door. She stood up as they came towards her and stepped into their path.

'So Mr.Tanner, we meet at last.'

Mary scrutinised the young couple as they sat down together in awkward silence.

'Can I get you a drink Mrs Cardew?' Steve plucked up the courage to make the first move.

'I'll have a tonic water.' Mary's tone radiated animosity.

'Coke for me please Steve,' said Sue nervously, noticing how Steve's colour rose as he turned away. This was not going to be easy.

Steve returned with the drinks, and Mary never spoke as he recounted the story of Lucy's accident. She could see it all, and her hatred of him began to diminish as she read the anguish in his eyes. It must have taken courage to confront reality in the way that he had, and his punishment was what he was going through now. It was the other girl, the one they refused to name, who Mary would hate forever.

'*Please* believe me Mrs Cardew,' said Sue, 'we really are most terribly sorry about what happened. It must be hard for you even to sit at the same table as us. But we'd like to keep in touch about Lucy, to know how things go, if you wouldn't mind that is.'

'I suppose that shows some slight spark of decency,' replied Mary, unable to keep the bitterness and sarcasm out of her voice. She looked at the brimming eyes in Sue's pink, honest face and felt a bitch.

'I'm sorry, that was unnecessary, but you must realise how hard it's been to come to terms with what's happened, and to discover that I'm capable of feeling such hatred. I suppose you could say that I've been emotionally cushioned all my life and it's easy to judge people when your own problems have never gone much beyond the price of milk and your son's obsession with irritating games.'

'Oh Mrs Cardew,' sniffed Sue, 'if only you knew what we would give for this never to have happened.'

'It never would have if you anti-hunt lot spent Saturdays doing something useful instead of victimising law-abiding people. Why do you people always have to make trouble and how much do you know about the ways of the country and hunting anyway?'

'I admit I know very little,' replied Steve, 'but I can't see that knowledge changes the fact that I think it's cruel to chase an animal with a pack of dogs. Cruelty is cruelty whatever way you look at it.'

'Don't you think that hunting is nearer to nature's way of predator and prey than the alternative methods of killing foxes and, make no mistake, they will be killed however much you lot bang on about animal rights. There's plenty of real cruelty going on in this country and if you really cared about animals, you would focus on that.'

'Steve and I haven't been sabbing since...' Sue paused, embarrassed, 'since that day,' she finished lamely.

Mary looked at her watch.

'We could argue all day and still end up like a television panel debate, with nobody listening to the other side and nobody answering any questions properly. You're as entitled to your opinions as I am to mine, but those who put the life of an animal above that of a child have no place in a civilised society.'

Mary stood up and tried to smile at the silent students.

'I must go, but I will let you know how Lucy goes on, I suppose I owe you that. Goodbye and thank you for coming.'

Steve held out his hand and, after a brief hesitation, Mary accepted it.

'Goodbye Mrs Cardew,' he said, 'I can only repeat how sorry we both are about what happened.'

Sue nodded dumbly, and they watched together as Mary left the pub. A sad figure walking briskly through the door and out into the street.

'Phew!' exclaimed Steve, 'I'm glad that's over – I could use the other half – you OK?'

'I wouldn't say no to a half shandy.'

Sue looked round the dingy, cluttered room. Reproduction horse brasses and an assortment of trinkets covered the yellowing walls, the air fusty with stale smoke and beer smells. One large, dismal log smouldered in the ash-filled grate, above which hung a cheap cork board, proudly displaying a collection of curling post-cards of silver sands, azure seas and the odd Eiffel Tower.

'Let's down these and go,' she suggested, as Steve returned with their drinks. 'I want to talk about it all, but this place is about as depressing as you can get.'

'Suits me. What did you think of her?'

'I don't really know, but I thought in the circumstances she wasn't too bad. I mean, I was worried she might get really abusive or hysterical and make an awful scene. D'you think she'll say anything to the police?'

'No...' Steve paused thoughtfully, 'I don't think so. I think she's understandably desperate to know what happened, but probably doesn't want any more trouble than she already has. Maybe I'm wrong – we'll have to wait and see.'

'I hope you're right, that's all I can say.'

Steve put down his empty glass and stood up ready to leave. 'Come on, let's go. I wonder whether she'll ever make contact to let us know about Lucy.'

'I think she will – and if she does, let's hope it's good news.'

*

'Mum!' shouted Ben, 'it's the hospital on the phone.'

Mary dropped the chopping knife she was using and rushed through to the office. Dread and hope gripped her in equal proportions as she picked up the receiver.

'Mrs Cardew? Oh hello, Dr Dawson speaking.'

Mary could tell nothing from the tone of his voice, which was as unemotional as always. Her heart began to thump as she screamed inside for him to hurry up.

'I have some encouraging news for you about Lucy. For the first time we have seen signs that the depth of coma is lightening and her response to external stimuli improving. I now believe that a gradual recovery is beginning.'

'Oh my God!' cried Mary, imminent tears pricking her eyeballs, '*tell me quickly*, how is she, will she be all right, when can we come.' The words rushed out with the tears. 'Hold on a minute. Ben, *Ben*!' she shouted, 'go and get Dad quick – sorry doctor, but I'm just, well – I don't know what to say.'

'Don't worry Mrs Cardew, I understand how you must feel.'

Like hell you do! thought Mary, but she was laughing now.

'Come to the hospital as soon as you wish, but I would like to see you both before you visit Lucy. There are one or two things I'd like to explain to you.'

'We shall be there as soon as we can and thank you – this is the best telephone call I've ever had in my life!'

Mary put down the telephone as Ted came in, closely followed by Ben. For once she did not notice he was still wearing his slurry encrusted gumboots and she flung herself into his arms as she gabbled out the news. They hugged each other, laughing and crying at the same time as they danced round the cluttered farm office, Ben looking on in amazement at his parents' peculiar behaviour.

'Can I come too?' he asked.

Mary broke away from Ted to embrace her embarrassed son.

'Of course you can. Lucy is just as much your sister as our daughter.'

Ben wriggled free and wiped his face where his mother's tears had mingled with her kiss. He was much too old to be kissed, thank goodness Freddie Williams had not witnessed the awful event.

'Come on Ted, we must hurry. We must be there when Lucy comes round.'

'Now steady love, steady. I'm as excited as you, but I don't think I'd be too welcome at the hospital smelling like this, neither do we know for sure how long it will be before she is completely conscious.' He hadn't the heart to tell his wife that it was possible she might not even recognise them.

'Oh Ted, who cares about your clothes, let's go now,

this minute.'

'Five minutes, that's all I need. Ben, go and shut the dogs up and turn off the barn lights. Mary, I smell burning, what's going on in the kitchen?'

Mary rushed to rescue the pan she had left on the stove, once the beginnings of a lamb hot-pot, but now only a burnt offering. She dumped it on the side, not caring a jot and ran to get the car out, unable to contain her impatience to be gone any longer.

Ted and Ben came out of the house together and she moved over into the passenger seat to let Ted drive as Ben jumped into the back.

She remembered the first time she had made the journey in the back of the ambulance, a journey she would never forget, and she prayed that this time it would herald the renaissance of her daughter's life.

When they reached the hospital, they were asked to wait in the same room where they had sat on that dreadful night, but Dr Dawson was with them in minutes, as if he knew that a long, agonising delay would be more than they could bear.

Three hopeful faces stared up at him as he entered the room, and he silently thanked some higher authority that the news, at least so far, was good.

'Why do you want to see us first?' asked Mary. 'Why can't we go straight in, there's nothing wrong is there?'

'Not at all Mrs. Cardew, Lucy is progressing nicely. Nevertheless, in order to avoid disappointment, there are certain things I think you should be aware of. As you know, Lucy has been on an artificial ventilator and therefore partly anaesthetised. She has been in a deep coma for nearly three weeks and her recovery will be gradual. I didn't want you to go in and expect to find your daughter sitting up in bed ready to greet you!'

'But how long will it be before she comes round properly?' asked Mary anxiously.

'That is a difficult question to answer accurately, as different people react in different ways. By this time tomorrow, we would expect her to be showing some signs of normal response to the world around her. Limb movements, recognition, that sort of thing, as the brain begins to work again in a demanding environment.'

'I think we understand that and can be patient for a little while longer,' said Ted, fearful that Mary might become discourteous in her eagerness to get on and see Lucy. 'Was there anything else you wanted to tell us?' he finished.

'Yes Mr Cardew – just one more thing that I think you should all be aware of. Injuries to the brain such as Lucy has suffered can result in long-term damage. It is impossible to tell at this stage whether or not this is the case, but I would be failing in my job if I did not point out the possibility.'

'What sort of things do you mean?' A cold hand clutched momentarily at Mary's rejoicing heart.

'Loss of memory, intellectual impairment, personality changes – even epilepsy is a possibility.'

There was a short silence, broken by Mary.

'But can't you tell, with all your scans and machines and things?'

'I'm afraid we can't entirely. As I think I explained to you before, CT, MRI scans or electroencephalograms only give a basic idea of what is going on. The progress of the patient is by far the most accurate way of predicting future prognosis. However, Lucy is young, she's strong and healthy and she's got all to play for. She also has a loving and supportive family and these are all important factors in her favour.'

'Can we see her now?' demanded Mary.

'I don't see why a short, quiet visit should do any harm, but please don't expect too much.'

'Would it be better if only her mother was to go in

today?' asked Ted. 'From what you say, I feel Ben and I should wait till tomorrow.'

'If you don't mind, Mr Cardew, I think that's a very sensible suggestion. Give her a bit more time to adjust to being back in the real world.'

'Oh Ted,' Mary squeezed his hand, 'are you sure?'

'Yes love, you go in now, Ben and I'll wait in the car and you can tell us everything on the way home.'

Mary walked steadily down the passage to the now familiar door and slowly pushed it open. The nurse, Rose, was sitting quietly watching Lucy and she smiled as Mary came in.

Mary's immediate reaction was one of crushing disappointment, for in spite of Dr Dawson's warning, she had still expected to see a change in Lucy. But here she was, looking exactly the same as she had since the accident.

Rose seemed to sense the woman's emotions and got up to put a hand on her shoulder.

'Don't worry Mrs Cardew, she's coming along nicely. Look at her carefully, there's a tiny touch of colour in her cheeks, and small movements that were not there before.'

Mary did as the nurse bade and after a few minutes, saw for herself that Rose was right. She picked up Lucy's limp hand and felt a slight movement in her fingers.

Her heart filled with joy and she bent forward to kiss her, as she always did. As she straightened up, Lucy's eyelids flickered briefly and then half-opened. The unfocused eyes stared at Mary for a second, then drooped shut again. Another second later, there was a tiny movement, and the faintest hint of a smile lifted the corners of her mouth.

'*She knew me*,' whispered Mary. 'Did you see, Rose – did you see? I *know* she knew me. God be thanked, she's going to be all right.'

*

'Steven Tanner?'

'Speaking.'

'It's Mary Cardew here.'

'Oh… hello.' Steve's heart lurched.

'I've got some good news – Lucy's regained consciousness. The doctors think she'll make a complete recovery given time.'

'*Thank goodness,*' Steve exhaled audibly with relief, 'Oh Mrs Cardew, I can't tell you what this means to me and Sue – we could never have forgiven ourselves if the worst had happened. Thank you for ringing and I promise we'll never trouble you again.'

Mary took a deep breath. 'Actually Steven, I don't want any more bitterness in my life. It wasn't you who frightened the pony, and I do believe you both feel real remorse. I've told Lucy about you and she said she'd like to meet you.'

Steve was gob-smacked. 'Well… um… I mean, are you sure you wouldn't mind? I know Sue would be pleased but…'

Mary cut in. 'No *buts* – I mean it. Life's too short for anger – forgiveness is a much better emotion. Anyway, at the moment, what Lucy wants she gets!'

'*Thank you.* We'd love to – it would mean the world to both of us.'

'Good. Ring me when you've spoken to Sue and we'll fix up a date.'

*

They had come to the farm, the pair of them, in the battered old coloured car. The atmosphere had been electric with nerves as Mary showed them into the kitchen, but her forgiveness had been complete. The tension evaporated as Ted, Ben and Lucy came in to greet them. Hands were shaken and the past finally consigned to a small corner of the memory cupboard.

Steve was fascinated by the farm and eagerly accepted

Ted's offer of a guided tour, leaving the girls to female chatter – Lucy being particularly keen to discuss university life with Sue. Bored by both, Ben disappeared to his room.

Lucy's accident had resulted in the forging of an unlikely bond between them all. Conscience and forgiveness had, in the end, overridden guilt and hatred, creating a friendship that none of them would ever have thought possible.

*

It was six months later, and Mary was hanging up laundry when the telephone rang. It was spring, the dark days had gone and new life was burgeoning on the land.

Mary ran in, dropping a sheet on the ground. Things like that never bothered her now. After what happened to Lucy, nothing as trivial as a dirty sheet was even worth a glance.

'Hello Mary, it's Steve. Sue and I were hoping we might drop in and see you all. We've got some news for you.'

'Yes, of course Steve. When were you thinking of? Lucy would love to see you if you could make it a week-end.'

'How about this Saturday sometime?'

'Fine, come to lunch. It's only a bit of a picnic but if you don't mind pot-luck, you're welcome.'

'Look forward to it and thanks – bye for now.'

*

Lucy had made remarkable progress since leaving hospital and had suffered no serious after-effects. Her speech was sometimes a little slurred and her concentration poor. She still tired easily, but there were no long-term worries about her condition. She loved to see Steve and Sue and was excited at the thought of their forthcoming visit.

'Well then, what's this news you two've come all this

way to tell us?' asked Ted, when the six of them were sitting round the kitchen table, washing the pot-luck down with a pint.

'I'm delighted to be able to tell you all that Sue has consented to be my wife – why I cannot imagine, but then she's always been a bit soft in the head!'

'Wonderful!' Mary and Ted exclaimed together.

'Brilliant!' Lucy cried, rushing round to kiss them. 'Can I be a bridesmaid?'

'Lucy, really!' laughed Mary. 'Seriously though, we couldn't be more pleased for you both – it's great news.'

Ben, worried he might be expected to kiss Sue, or worse still be kissed, asked if he could go.

'Freddie's coming over after lunch. We're going fishing and I want to get my tackle ready.'

'Off you go then,' said Ted, 'but don't be late, it's your turn to feed the orphan lambs.'

'OK Dad,' groaned Ben. 'Bye,' he waved at Steve and Sue before hurrying out to be ready for his friend.

'When's the happy day?' continued Mary.

'We haven't fixed a date yet, but it won't be for ages I guess. We'd like to get jobs and somewhere to live sorted if possible before taking the plunge.'

'The sooner the better,' beamed Sue, who had finally discovered why her friends all raved about sex.

'This calls for a celebration,' announced Ted, and he disappeared into the larder, reappearing a moment later with a bottle of sparkling wine.

'Not the real thing I'm afraid but it'll do. Fetch some glasses Mary, and we'll drink a toast.'

The cork popped and the wine fizzed into the waiting glasses.

'To Sue and Steve – the very best of luck for your future together.'

Mary, Ted and Lucy raised their glasses and drank, Lucy spluttering as the bubbles went up her nose.

'Our thanks and here's to you all too, especially you, Lucy,' replied Steve, raising his glass specifically to her.

Later, when all the excitement had died down and it was time to leave, Steve went to find Mary, who had gone to the office. She glanced up from a heap of papers as he came in.

'You two off now? I won't be a minute.'

'There's something I want to tell you, Mary. The girl, the one we wouldn't name. Her name was Gita, Gita Taverner.'

'It doesn't matter any longer, Steve. It's all in the past now and best left there.

But Steve insisted on continuing, 'I thought you should know, she was involved in a car smash three weeks ago and suffered serious head injuries. They said there was little or no chance of her recovering, so her parents ordered the life support machine to be turned off.'

Mary sat down with a plonk on the old desk chair.

'She's dead then?'

'Yes, she died on Thursday. We lived together once you see, so I was told all about it by a uni friend.'

'I didn't know that Steve, I'm sorry.'

'I don't think Gita was ever meant to be happy – she was always at war with the world and herself somehow.'

'Do you believe in retribution, Steve?'

'No Mary, I don't, and I don't believe you do either.'

'We'll never know, will we, but it's not something to dwell on anyway. Come on, you two must go. The Vicarys are coming to supper and Lucy needs a rest before Poppy comes whirl-winding in. There're potatoes to be peeled, cows to be milked, and Ben and Freddie to cope with as well.'

She kissed Steve quickly and smiling, gently pushed him out.

'It's the future we've all got to think about now, not the past, and that's the way it should be.'

BOOK FOUR: PINK GIN AND DOG HAIRS

Looking back on it, I suppose it was one of the stranger interludes in my life and, as so many things do, it all began with a chance meeting.

I had not seen Linkey Amberly for nearly 30 years until that fateful day when I was sitting waiting for a friend to join me for lunch in a little known restaurant in Kensington.

As I glanced round the slightly tatty room, I noticed a woman of about my age, also alone, staring at me. As I caught her eye, she looked away and pretended to fuss with her handbag, eventually producing a packet of cigarettes and a cheap throwaway lighter. I watched covertly as she glanced around the room and seeing no other smokers, replaced the cigarettes in her bag, a brief look of something between annoyance and resignation crossing her face.

The tiniest tinkle of a bell rang somewhere in my mind but at that moment my friend rushed in and I forgot all about the lone stranger on the other side of the room.

We ordered our food and chatted away and it was not until we were drinking our coffee that I noticed the woman staring at me once again, when I jokingly asked my friend if there was anything peculiar about my appearance. Having been assured that I looked perfectly normal, we returned to our conversation and I suppressed the small prickle of irritation that had begun to creep into my soul, for I disliked being the object of unsolicited scrutiny.

My friend suddenly looked at her watch and jumped up. She had to *dash*, as she put it, or she'd be late for an appointment with her solicitor who was sorting out her rather messy divorce.

I was in no hurry and having said my farewells, settled back to finish my coffee. Almost immediately, the staring woman got up and crossed the room to where I was sitting. She stood looking down at me, a broad smile on her face.

'It *is* you isn't it, Rosie Crossley?' she said. 'I'm Linkey, Linkey Amberly from Foxgrove, don't you remember?'

For a moment, my brain stalled and I was too amazed to answer; there in front of me stood my best friend from preparatory school. The friend with whom I had shared so much and to whom I had sworn lifelong loyalty and devotion. We had even pricked fingers and mingled two very small drops of blood.

How she had recognised me, and what extraordinary chance had brought us both to the same place at the same time nearly three decades on, I could not imagine. Yet suddenly this middle-aged woman was Linkey and as the years fell away, she became once more the wild, laughing 11 year-old from whom I had parted at the end of that last summer term at Foxgrove Preparatory School for Girls.

Of course we sat down together and ordered more coffee to celebrate our incredible meeting. It was wonderful to see Linkey again and she seemed equally pleased to see me, and as we chatted and reminisced our laughter grew louder, turning a few heads in the restaurant.

We had both turned forty and somehow, as age creeps on, the past becomes a thing of value to be re-explored and delighted in. Death becomes a reality from which we are no longer mysteriously exempt, and as the circle turns, childhood memories seem precious and reassuring. Linkey had filled a great deal of my early life and, with our chance meeting, the clock had spun backwards as if its spring had gone mad.

We talked and talked until we were politely asked to leave, for the staff wanted to begin preparing for the evening, and those who remained were looking decidedly glum.

We swapped details and parted with resolutions to keep in touch and meet again in the near future. If we let another such chunk of our lives pass, it was possible that we would only meet again in heaven.

As it turned out, it was to be nearly six months before we did meet, for I had been away in Tanzania, visiting my ageing parents. They still lived on the farm where I had been brought up under the gaze of Mount Kilimanjaro. The flight back to London had been a nightmare journey of delays and diversions, and I was worried about the situation in Africa. I felt exhausted and had gone to bed early when the telephone rang.

It was Linkey, inviting me down to Devon, where she now lived, to spend a few days catching up on old times and renewing our friendship. It was really more of a royal command than an invitation, which made me smile, for Linkey's direct and breezy approach to life had always been hard to resist and she had obviously not changed.

I was a moderately successful freelance journalist and having no particular assignment to work on at the moment, my time was my own and I accepted her invitation with alacrity. London in November held little charm for me, as the Christmas festivities had not yet begun and spring seemed far away.

I had hardly given a thought to what life had thrown at Linkey since leaving Foxgrove, for in spite of our youthful blood-sisterhood, our paths had led us in very different directions and we had soon lost touch completely.

My hazy memories of visits to the Amberly home during the school holidays were of a standard middle-class country family. Everyone seemed happy and busy, spending as much time as possible outdoors, and the house was comfortable in a rather scruffy, chaotic way.

Linkey's father, Captain Amberly, was a kindly but shy man who preferred the peace of his study and *The Times* crossword to his daughter's noisy friends. He had been at sea for most of his naval career, but by the time I met him he was working at the Admiralty in London and we saw little of him.

Mrs Amberly was a brisk, straightforward woman who guided her children's upbringing with an admirable blend of tolerance and coercion which resulted in few rows and much laughter. Linkey had two older brothers, three dogs, a menagerie of small nursery creatures and a couple of ponies, all of which made up the family.

The brothers considered us beneath consideration, but the dogs and ponies were more forthcoming and we spent most of our time galloping around the common near where they lived, shrieking and falling off, much to the delight of the dogs who would rush up and lick our faces as we lay laughing helplessly in the heather.

The ponies were decent enough not to gallop off and we always returned home safely, in spite of never wearing hard hats or understanding about a strange man, who occasionally appeared from behind gorse bushes brandishing a large sausage from beneath his raincoat.

I suppose looking back on it all, Linkey was a rather wild and wayward child but her personality, like her mother's, was completely straightforward and open. I doubt that she was ever much troubled by the complexes and uncertainties endured by many of us during the tiresome process of growing up.

But that was all in the past, and now I looked forward eagerly to my forthcoming visit to Wellshead, the charmingly named house in Devon where Linkey now lived. There was so much to catch up on after all those years. Although we had talked endlessly in the restaurant, all our talk had been of old times and we had not got beyond school days before we were booted out.

Consequently I had no idea whether Linkey was married, had been married, had children or what.

I packed a case with what I considered to be a suitable wardrobe for a few days in the country and with a feeling of childish excitement, slammed the front door and set off on the long drive west.

The journey seemed to take forever, as the traffic was bad leaving London and there were the inevitable road works on the motorway. Luckily the scrawled directions and home-made map that Linkey had sent me were faultless and I arrived at Wellshead without getting lost, just as dusk was changing rapidly to dark.

The house was at the end of a long narrow lane, the surface of which gradually deteriorated into more pot-holes than tarmac. The rain had started to fall, and peering through the windscreen, all I could see were dark beech hedges, rearing up out of high grass covered banks, with dying ferns tumbling over the edge of the lane.

As I swung into the drive, the welcoming lights of Wellshead shone through the rain, and as I drew up at the front door, relief swept over me.

I tooted twice, but Linkey must have been watching out for my arrival for within seconds, the door was flung open and there she stood, silhouetted against the light from inside.

A tide of dogs streamed out over the threshold and as I stepped out of the car they seemed to engulf me with their greeting. 'Welcome, Rosie – you've made it!' cried Linkey. 'Push those wretched dogs down, here you lot get back in the house,' she shouted at the dogs, who surprisingly obeyed her command, clearing a path for Linkey and I to greet each other properly, and to quickly haul my luggage out of the car into the dry of the hall. The dogs stood watching, tails waving slowly, keen critical eyes summing up the new and unfamiliar arrival.

'It's wonderful to see you,' she said, 'I've been looking

forward so much to this visit. I hope you've brought some warm clothes, most people seem to think this house is freezing.'

She stood and looked at me, head cocked on one side rather like a long-legged bird. 'You didn't grow much then, did you? You know you haven't changed a day, hardly even a wrinkle. Still the same clean, neat little Rosamund Crossly,' she smiled with genuine pleasure, briefly touching my shoulder in a gesture of affection.

I laughed at her remarks which were so typical of the Linkey I remembered. Always straight and to the point yet completely without rancour or spite, and it was impossible to take offence. 'Come on, you must be tired,' and grabbing my cases she strode off towards the staircase, closely attended by the dogs. I followed on behind, scarcely able to see my way in the dim glow that lit the stairwell.

We all tramped along an equally dim passage, and eventually arrived at the end where Linkey kicked open an old oak door. 'Here we are,' she announced, switching on a light and dumping my luggage on the floor beside an old four-poster bed. 'Do you want to unpack now or have tea or what? Supper is usually about eight.'

'I'd love a cup of tea,' I answered and we all trooped off downstairs again and along more passages until finally we arrived in the kitchen.

An ancient cream *AGA* dominated the room, giving out a warmth so far lacking in the other parts of the house I had visited. The only concession to modernity was a strip light which provided a welcome relief from the gloom of the rest of Wellshead. An immensely fat black and white cat lay sleeping on a pile of old magazines beside the *AGA*, and even the clamour of our arrival failed to rouse it from its slumbers.

A big pine table stood in the middle of the room, surrounded by wheelback chairs, and I selected the nearest possible place to the *AGA* and sat down, at last allowing a sense of ease and relaxation to flow over me.

As the kettle began its slow ascent to boiling and Linkey pottered about fetching milk and making toast, I was able to take stock of my old friend. She was wearing a pair of filthy old jeans with holes beginning to appear at the knees and a blue sweater of similar decrepitude. The back of the sweater resembled an abandoned bird's nest with pieces of hay and dog hairs forming a mat with the fibres of the thick furry wool. Her wavy chestnut hair showed few signs of grey, nor the attentions of a brush or comb, and makeup was clearly not something she bothered with. She was tall and thin as she always had been and moved with an easy grace, but there was a certain tension and restlessness in her which had not been there in childhood.

I thought, with humour, of the very different picture I must present for I knew myself to be a neat and precise sort of person who could not stand a hair out of place, either about my person or in my house. I briefly envied Linkey her insouciance but knew I could never be happy with her way, anymore than she with mine.

I looked at the dogs stretched out on the floor in front of the *AGA*, my chair an island in the middle of a sea of fawn and grey. Linkey must have read my thoughts, as when the tea finally arrived on the table and she sat down, she said 'I hope you don't mind the dogs, I'm afraid they will shed a few hairs on your immaculate clothes – I should have warned you to bring only grey or beige garments!' 'I don't mind at all,' I replied untruthfully, 'I like dogs. Anyway what are they and what are they all called?' 'Those three great big things with the whiskery faces are Scottish Deerhounds called Brodie, Teasel and Minstrel, and the two fawn ones are lurchers called Slipper and Mustard. I never meant to have so many but somehow they just kept arriving.'

I didn't inquire from whence the dogs had kept arriving and let this rather bizarre statement go by.

'Come on, wade into the toast before I eat it all. You're not on a diet or anything ridiculous like that are you? I'm constantly starving in the winter.' So saying, Linkey demolished several slices of toast and jam before sitting back with a contented sigh, a mug of steaming tea on the table in front of her.

'Well as you were always so fond of pointing out, I'm a short-arse and not a beanpole and we short-arses have to watch the pounds in middle age.' I cut the one remaining slice of toast in half, breaking my resolution to give up tea and nibbles forever.

Linkey whipped a packet of cigarettes out of her jeans pocket and lit up, blowing smoke up at the ceiling. 'I suppose the old fags help keep the weight down but they certainly don't suppress my appetite.' She reached for the last half slice of toast, dropping ash into the sugar bowl on the way.

'I thought tonight we would have a quiet kitchen supper and a real good catch up chat and I expect you'd like a fairly early night. The air here is quite different to London you know and most people find it makes them sleepy. Tomorrow I've asked a few friends to dinner to entertain you, some down off the moor and some from the village. I owe them and of course they are all dying to inspect my old friend from the past.'

'Honestly Linkey, you shouldn't have bothered. I've come down here to see you and have a rest from the London whirl. I won't be in the least bit bored if we do nothing special at all.' I felt rather nervous at the thought of Linkey's friends coming *down off the moor* to peer at me. It sounded as if they lived in a hole in the ground and probably wore skins. 'Besides, Linkey, I'm not a state registered object of curiosity you know. Who on earth are these strange moorland dwellers anyway, do they speak with foreign tongue and have hairy feet?'

'Good gracious no! They're called Sidebottom but they like it to be pronounced *Siddibotome* if you please – I'm afraid they're a bit boring but harmless – they're on a sort of good-life kick which I suspect won't last long.'

'Why do you bother with them then?'

'I don't really know to be honest, except that they're both so well-meaning I suppose I feel sorry for them in a way. Perhaps they're part of my very small social conscience. Apart from £2 a month to Oxfam and Cancer Research I don't do anything much to help those less fortunate than myself.'

Here she stopped and giggled. 'Do you remember how Miss Ogle used to go on about being nice to those less fortunate than yourself and what a silly old fool we used to think she was? Do you realise she was probably 30 at the most and we used to wonder how she could still be alive, she seemed so ancient.'

I, too, giggled, a thing I hadn't done in years, for I remembered it all only too well. Linkey was always inciting me to play noughts and crosses during Miss Ogle's lessons, which usually ended up with me getting into trouble for I was not half as good as Linkey at covering my tracks.

'Anyway,' she continued, 'as I said, I owe them and as they came from some grim London suburb, I thought you might be able to help the conversation along a bit.'

'Thanks a lot! It's so good to see you, you always did make me laugh which is worth all the rest of you I suppose, but right now I could murder a hot bath and a chance to get my things unpacked. My back's like a board from the drive.'

'Oh goodness! I hadn't thought about hot water. I never seem to bath much in the winter. I often intend to but never quite seem to get round to it. My bathroom's freezing and if the generator has a tantrum the water is too.'

My heart sank as I realised that the muffled thumping noise in the background that I was going to ask about, must in fact be the generator. Trust Linkey to live in a house with no mains electricity.

'Don't worry, give me 20 minutes and all will be well.' Before I could answer she disappeared.

I remained in my chair by the *AGA* and spoke to the dogs who appeared to have accepted me on their mistress's behalf, but were totally indifferent to my overtures. One, I think Teasel, thumped its tail in a vaguely gratifying way but the others slept on along with the cat.

A nice long case clock with a brass face ticked steadily away in the corner and somewhere outside in the dark an owl hooted. The rain tapped on the kitchen windows, blown against the panes by the gusting wind. My eyelids were drooping and my tea growing cold when Linkey burst back into the room and all the dogs jumped up.

'Everything is now ready for you, madam,' she announced, 'would you like to take a drink up? The sun's well over the yardarm and when I've got you settled and fed the dogs I shall certainly open the bar and have my usual.'

'What on earth's your *usual* – and no thanks – I don't drink much at all. Maybe a glass of vino at dinner or an apple juice or something.'

'Good God! *Vino*, how terribly SW something – and this may be Devon but there ain't no apple juice around here. Plenty of grape though. As to my usual, you may remember my father was an old sea dog and I was brought up on pink gin.'

'Absolute rubbish Linkey, your parents would never have dreamt of letting you drink gin when you were a child.'

'Too true,' she agreed, 'but nevertheless, it *is* my tipple now and I do rather enjoy it. It's funny don't you think, how when we were young we always said we'd never be like our parents? Things like wearing those dreadful hats our mothers did and lots of other things. Yet in grown-up life the subconscious influence of their habits and ideals has seeped into our being and helped shape us into what we have become. In my case a pink ginner.'

'What is pink gin anyway?'

'You are ignorant – it's gin with a dash of *Angostura*, though I have tonic as well to make it last longer.'

'Sounds disgusting. Come on, let's go up. I'm dying to wash away London and ease my stiffening bones.'

She readily agreed and led me back through the long passages and up the staircase to my room.

It was a wonderful revelation. A fire burned brightly in the small grate and the lamps seemed to have taken on a new lease of life, bathing the room in a warm light. The curtains were drawn and the bed turned down and two plainly visible lumps under the patchwork cover proclaimed hot water bottles.

Next door in the bathroom an ancient geezer was belching out steaming water into an enormous bath with a mahogany rail running round the edge. Bubbles frothed under its rusty spout and a delicious smelling vapour filled the room, misting up the tiny mirror over the basin.

'Oh Linkey,' I cried, 'what luxury – I won't be long.'

'Be as long as you like, there's no hurry at all so make the most of it. The Old Trout's left something in the oven so I really don't care when we eat. I'm off now to do a few things that need doing, so see you downstairs when you feel like it.' She swung out of the room, heading eagerly no doubt for the gin bottle. Who The Old Trout was, had yet to be revealed, but I assumed her to be some good domestic whom I should probably meet in the morning.

It must have been well over an hour later when I finally groped my way back downstairs to join Linkey.

All the generator's energy seemed to have gone into my quarters for the rest of the house was as dim and gloomy as ever. The kitchen was empty, but I was pleased to notice two saucepans simmering away on the hob. I wandered back into the hall and, noticing some light shining under a door at the end of a short passage that led off the hall, followed its beam and pushed open the door.

Linkey was sitting in a wing back chair beside a blazing log fire, cigarette in hand and a glass at her elbow. She appeared to be doing *The Times* crossword and was still wearing the same old clothes as when I arrived. I noticed that she wore no spectacles but could tell, from the way she was holding the paper, that they would soon be needed.

For a brief moment it could have been her father sitting there and I, once again, a small nervous child, peeping round the door to see if it was safe to enter. For all her bravado, Linkey was much in awe of Captain Amberly and treated him with great respect.

Linkey looked up as I came in and smiled. 'Ooh, you do look smart, I'm afraid I change as seldom as possible, which is never unless people are coming. Push those dogs off and find a space on the sofa. Have a good bath?'

'Wonderful thanks, I feel a new woman and might even go mad and join you in a small drink before we eat.'

'Excellent – I'll get the wine – won't be a minute. Can't do the bloody puzzle today anyway, my brain must be collapsing, not enough gin probably!' With that she picked up her near empty glass, drained it and left the room.

I cannot even understand *The Times* crossword, let alone do it and I hoped she would abandon it now I had arrived. I sat as close to the fire as the dogs allowed, for the room, like the rest of the house, was cold. I began to understand Linkey's reluctance to change her clothes for there is no better way to keep warm than to preserve existing body heat. Perhaps she even slept in them with all the dogs on the bed as a sort of substitute electric blanket. Probably not, I decided, for that would be going too far, even for her.

I glanced around the room, noticing as I did so some beautiful antique furniture, struggling to make its presence felt among the clutter of old magazines and miscellaneous boxes overflowing with papers. Everything about the room was old and tatty and the condition of the paintwork and furnishings deplorable. It had obviously all been good once, but once had been a long time ago.

I thought of my own sitting room where nothing was out of place and the furniture gleamed against its background of pristine apricot walls which blended contentedly with the heavy silk curtains. How strongly houses reflect the character of their owners, and how strange that the two very different people we had grown into could be such good friends.

A grand piano stood in one corner, the top covered in photographs. Linkey had certainly never shown any interest in music that I could recall and I wondered where it had come from. As Linkey had not returned, I got up to inspect the photographs and noticed that the piano was a Steinway. How or why Linkey had acquired such a valuable instrument I could not imagine. Why hadn't she sold it and put the house onto mains electricity.

I was intrigued by the photographs and found pictures of Captain and Mrs Amberly, their old home and people on horses. Also of Linkey herself receiving a trophy from a Mr Blobby lookalike. I presumed this to be a point-to-point racing prize as the background was filled with gumbooted folk, plenty of mud and a slightly cock-eyed tent or two.

Amongst this crowd of nostalgia, and looking rather out of place, rested a large silver frame containing a formal studio portrait of an incredibly good-looking young man.

I wracked my brains to try and recall the faces of Linkey's brothers, but I had hardly known them and it was all too long ago. I was sure, though, that they had been fair haired, whereas the mystery man was dark and had a brooding look which I could not associate with any member of the carefree Amberly clan.

As I returned to my place by the fire Linkey came back into the room carrying a tray with our two full glasses, a plate of anchovies on toast and a bowl of green olives.

'How delicious, I love anchovies and olives!' I took my glass of wine, 'I shan't need any supper after this.'

'Well I shall,' she replied, plonking down in her chair and eating several olives before lighting up the inevitable cigarette. She gestured vaguely with her hand towards the small table where she had put the tray. 'Help yourself, we've only got cottage pie and a bit of cheese and I shouldn't like you to go to bed hungry on your first night.'

'I don't know where you put it all, Linkey. You're as thin as a stick yet you eat like a horse.'

'Metabolism,' she replied, 'it's all to do with energy and burning it off you know. Or perhaps I've got worms – I worm all the animals but never myself!'

'Oh Linkey,' I laughed, 'it's so typical of you to say something revolting like that, will you never change!'

'I hope not and most unlikely, I'm quite happy as I am. Seriously though, none of us really change you know. Obviously our bodies change and little bits of our personality can be changed by the things that happen to us but deep down, your soul is the soul that you are born with and will die with. Do you remember at school when Mary Callingham's father died and we were all told to be nice to her?'

'I do vaguely but what's that got to do with it?'

'Well,' continued Linkey, now in full flow, 'I remember thinking how awful for her but I couldn't imagine what it must have been like. I thought that when I was old and my parents died, I would somehow have changed inside so that it wouldn't really matter very much – that grown-ups had a kind of immunity to grief just because of their age. But of course it did, it mattered terribly and I realised then that my inner being was mine for life, and that there would never be any convenient shield to hide behind to lessen grief and adversity.'

There was really no answer to this, so I murmured my agreement and had a sip of wine. 'Tell me Linkey, who's the good looking man on the piano? That's not one of your brothers is it?'

'Good heavens no, that's David Maxwell, my ex. We were married for about five years. I'd forgotten I hadn't mentioned that little episode in my life but it was all so long ago now that I seldom give it a thought.'

'But Linkey, you still call yourself Amberly and no wedding ring do I espy.'

She shrugged and a shuttered look crossed her face. 'It's not a thing I particularly want to remember. I don't know why I keep that photograph but somehow it just seems to stay there. David gave me that piano, you see, for a wedding present so I suppose it's a sort of memorial to what might have been. Why on earth he gave it to me I can't imagine because he knew I'd never play it, but his father gave it to his mother who did play, and they had a long and happy marriage. Poor David, I think he saw the wretched piano as a sort of talisman. We did have some good times but we were young and silly and it just didn't work out.'

'I'm sorry, I didn't realise. Would it be tactless to ask what went wrong?'

'No, not at all. I blame my upbringing to some extent. You know, all that precious virginity rubbish and not sleeping around. It's laughable today but I suppose our poor mothers were conditioned only ever to sleep with one man and produce children, and I can only hope they were happy. But David stole my virginity, entirely with my agreement I may say, and sex came into my life like the March wind. We just couldn't get enough of it, and I thought it meant we would love each other until death did us part and thereto we plighted our troth. Not a sound basis for marriage.'

'It must have been a horrid time for you though.'

'Yes... I suppose so. Trouble was, he loved me too much – I couldn't cope. Being loved is a great responsibility you know.'

I got the impression that Linkey's marriage was not a subject for further discussion, and although I would love to have known more about it, it was not my business to inquire.

'How about you,' she asked after a brief silence, 'I presume you never tied the knot?'

'You presume correctly. I was very tempted with someone called Philip Winslade but by the time he came along I was nearly 30 and had life pretty well organised with house, job and all that and I couldn't really see the point in upsetting it all. I know that sounds callous and I did love him but not enough, I suppose, to sacrifice my independence.'

'Oh dear, was the poor man heartbroken or anything exciting like that?'

'Not in the least, he was married within 3 months to a rather dreary girl called Amanda someone or other and as far as I know lived happily ever after.'

Linkey laughed and the strained look that had come over her face when we spoke of her marriage vanished as quickly as it had come. 'Honestly,' she said, 'we were pretty poor examples of the swinging 60s immorality and freedom, you and I. I've made up for it since though. Imagine going to one's grave having only sampled one man. I enjoy sex anyway so why not indulge? It's rather like a really good bottle of Burgundy!'

'I suppose that's one way of looking at it,' I replied, 'but what about now, do you still indulge, as you put it?'

'The flesh is willing but the opportunities lacking I fear.'

'What about the estimable Mr. Sidebottom – do I detect a secret liaison under the myopic eye of our Eileen?'

I tried to keep a straight face but Linkey's shriek was too much and we fell about laughing at the thought. 'Oh Rosie!' she gasped, 'wait till you see him tomorrow night and for heaven's sake don't catch my eye or I shall have hysterics. He's quite gruesome and probably needs to be tied up and whipped by a thigh-booted Eileen to get it up at all.'

'Poor Mr. Sidebottom, my friend Linkey thinks you're kinky!'

'Shut up Rosie – stop making me laugh – my stomach's hurting and you'll set off my smoker's cough. Come on, let's go and eat before The Old Trout's pie dries up or I have another pinkey.' As she had already had at least three *pinkeys* as she called her tipple, and dried up cottage pie was not my favourite, I readily agreed and we wandered back to the kitchen preceded by the dogs.

The food was delicious and by 11 o'clock we were both yawning. The fire in the sitting room was a heap of dying embers and the only chance of warmth seemed to lie in my bedroom. I thanked Linkey for a lovely evening and bade her good night.

'Sleep well,' she replied, 'I've only got to do the dogs and then I shall be up too. Don't forget if you need a light in the night use the torch or you'll upset the generator. I get up rather early but lie-in as long as you like.' She disappeared down a dark passage, the dogs rushing excitedly on ahead, toe nails clicking on the old tiles.

I had no need for the torch as I slept the sleep of the dead and awoke to find it was after 8 o'clock. I couldn't believe I had slept for so long for I was not normally a particularly good sleeper. Obviously the Devon air had got me in its grip as Linkey suggested it might. I was quite happy about that and stretched out in the warmth and comfort of my bed. I decided to have a good read, a luxury I seldom enjoyed at home where I always felt guilty about getting up late.

I was deep in the heart of Mongolia when there was a knock on the door and before I could answer, it swung open and a strange little woman carrying a tray walked in. She was not much above 5ft and could have been any age between 60 and 80 and was undoubtedly The Old Trout.

'I've brought you a cup of tea,' she said, in what I presumed to be a broad Devon accent. '*She's* outside but there's breakfast in the kitchen when you like.' She slapped the tray down on a table by the window and tore back the curtains, her small ageing body radiating a kind of terrifying energy and toughness that I imagined was wholly necessary if you *did* for Linkey.

She turned and scrutinised me for a moment, hand on hip. 'I'm Mrs Trouton by the way and pleased to see you I be. She doesn't have enough friends by half.' With that she scuttled out of the room before I had time to stammer out my thanks, leaving me with the impression that in her mind people who lay in bed were sinful but that as I was a friend of her mistress, I had passed her stringent test of acceptability.

As I would have to get out of bed to fetch the tea, I decided to abandon my lie-in and set about the day ahead. A blanket of fog obscured most of the view but at least the rain had stopped and there was a chance that the fog would lift. Out of bed, the room was stone cold and I dressed quickly in the warmest clothes I had, sipping gratefully at Mrs Trouton's welcome cup of tea.

I was rather annoyed to notice that all my clothes from last night were covered in dog hairs, and I folded them up to take downstairs in the hopes the house might yield a clothes brush.

As I passed through the hall, I heard sounds of tuneless singing coming from a room I had not yet visited, and a closer inspection revealed Mrs Trouton feverishly polishing a large oak refectory table in preparation, I presumed, for the forthcoming dinner party.

'Shan't be long,' she said, as she glanced up and saw me standing in the doorway. 'I'll be doing you some breakfast.'

'Oh please don't worry,' I replied, 'I only ever have toast and coffee and I'm sure I can manage by myself, I can see you're busy. I would love a clothes brush sometime though, if you have one.'

She tut-tutted at the thought of someone not eating a proper cooked breakfast and stood watching me, tightly permed grey head nodding. 'That'll be the dog hairs I suppose, you leave those things to me and I'll fetch them up for you.' Before I could protest, she grabbed the clothes out of my hands and beetled off towards the kitchen.

By the time I'd had my toast and coffee there was still no sign of Linkey, so I decided to explore the house and see what further it could tell me about my friend and her life. Mrs Trouton clearly had plenty to do and in order to keep out of her way I chose the upstairs as my starting point.

There were several doors to be opened, mostly revealing unused bedrooms of no great interest. All had the same shabby air about them as the rest of the house, and brown patches of damp stained the walls in many places. I shivered as I closed the last door and felt thankful that I'd not been allocated any of these particular rooms.

A small half-landing with three doors leading off it remained to be explored. I pushed open the first of these and smiled, for I'd obviously found Linkey's room. Clothes lay all over the place in untidy heaps, and the little amount of remaining floor space was taken up by two large dog beds and a pile of books. A dilapidated rabbit wearing a red waistcoat sat on the pillows in the middle of the double bed, his drooping ear and missing eye giving him a forlorn and sad appearance.

I closed the door, suddenly feeling like an intruder who had no business to be there, and tried the last two rooms. The first was small and completely empty although some faded curtains still hung at the window and a threadbare carpet covered most of the floor. The walls were dotted with x-hooks and brown squares showed where many small pictures had once hung. I thought it had probably been a man's dressing room and the hooks the bearers of school or regimental photographs, but the stale, musty air that hit me when I opened the door proclaimed years of disuse.

The third door was locked. At first, imagining it to be stuck, I shoved my shoulder against it but there was no give, so I gave up and set off back downstairs to the kitchen.

Linkey had come back in and was sitting at the kitchen table drinking coffee and arguing in a light-hearted way with Mrs Trouton.

'Morning Rosie,' she raised a hand in greeting, 'hope you slept well. Naughty old Trouty says you were making a fuss about the dog hairs! She's being very tiresome about dinner tonight and tells me we've got to go into town for some candles and things so we'd better go or I shall be in the dog house.'

'I should think so too Mrs Maxwell,' sniffed the old woman, 'and I shall be needing some more eggs if you don't mind.'

'Ooh Trouty, we are in a grump!' laughed Linkey, turning to me. 'Trouty only calls me Mrs Maxwell when she's in a mood – she knows I hate it.'

'It's your name it be when all's done and said,' she snapped back. Grabbing a handful of dusters she huffed off out of the room. It was obviously quite normal for the two of them to bicker in this way, and I suspected that they had known each other for a very long time.

'What does she usually call you then?' I asked.

'Miss Lavinia of course, she's known me since I was a baby.'

'Heavens, I'd quite forgotten your real name is Lavinia – the only person I ever heard call you that was your father.'

'Yes, dear old Dad, he hated nicknames and I was named after his favourite sister who died when she was ten of some dreadful disease or other. I suppose in those days it was much easier to die. Come on, let's go. Got a coat?'

Without giving me time to answer, we jumped into Linkey's Land Rover and roared off to the local town. The vehicle was ancient, and we rattled and banged at high speed along single track roads and round blind bends. By some miracle we made it and stopped with a jolt in the main square.

Any of the passing folk would have looked at home in the mud and rain of Linkey's point-to-point photograph, and I half expected to find sheep queuing in the shops. The town was an attractive little market town, and I would have loved to have stayed longer and had a wander around but Linkey seemed to be in a great hurry. We made our purchases, greeted a few people in passing and returned to the Land Rover.

'Could we possibly go a bit slower on the way back?' I asked bravely.

'What on earth for?' demanded Linkey as she gunned the engine. 'Apart from anything else, the sun's well over the yardarm and I need my pinkey.'

'I don't think there is any sun in Devon,' I replied, 'or is that because it's permanently over this famous yardarm?'

Linkey laughed as we swung out of the square. 'Well done, Rosie, you're getting the hang of things at last,' she shouted over the noise of the engine, 'but I will go slowly so you can view the fine Devon countryside in all its foggy glory.' She reduced speed which not only calmed my nerves, but enabled us to have a normal conversation.

'Tell me about Wellshead,' I asked. 'How long have you lived here?'

'Oh ages. I was very lucky really, I inherited it. You wouldn't remember Aunt Clarice Abbot, but she was a spinster aunt of my mother's and this was her family home. She had a younger sister but neither of them ever married. Mum told me once that all their boyfriends were killed in the '14-18 war so it was rather sad really.'

'But why didn't she leave it to your elder brother?'

'Luckily for me she favoured the female of the species, and by the time she was old and sorting out her affairs Martin and Victor were both well on their way in life. Neither of them had anything in common with her anyway. I adored her, actually, although some people thought her slightly batty.'

I smiled to myself at this remark, imagining that in old age Linkey could well be equally batty, although eccentric would probably be a kinder way of putting it. Whether or not she would live that long with her pink gins and cigarettes remained to be seen.

'Go on,' I said. 'What about Mrs. Trouton, where does she fit in?'

'Ah, The Old Trout was Aunt C's sort of maid of all works so of course has known me forever. She's been at Wellshead all her life you know. Her father was the gardener and her mother the cook and her family have been here forever. She has her own cottage in the village which Aunt C left her and a bit of money too. Old

Trouton fell off a tractor and died and her only offspring, a simply vile specimen called Royston, went to the big city and married a tart. They never bother with her or she with them. Wellshead is her life and because I happen to live here, I am too. I shall look after her for ever one way or another, I couldn't do without her anyway.'

We bounced over the pot-holes and jolted up to the back door where the dogs were waiting to greet us. 'Here we are,' said Linkey unnecessarily and jumped out of the Land Rover into the usual sea of fur and waving tails. 'Bring the rest of the things could you, I must have a pee.' *And a pinkey*, I thought.

I had wanted to ask about the locked door, but the opportunity had never arisen and I was left to speculate on the mystery room of Wellshead. There was probably some terribly boring explanation but my curiosity was aroused, for judging by the architecture of the house, this was no small box room but a substantial chamber. My questions would have to wait.

The rest of the day seemed to fly past and before I knew it, the time had come to think about getting ready for the evening. Linkey had told me not to dress up as she did not have formal parties, neither did she have the time or inclination to *tart herself up*, as she put it.

However, it was totally alien to me not to take trouble with my appearance, so I went in search of Linkey to tell her of my intentions. I found her in the old dairy arranging some cheese on a board ready for dinner. 'Hi,' she greeted me, eating a piece of Stilton, 'this is the only job I'm allowed to do, The Old Trout thinks I'm incapable of doing anything else.'

'I'm delighted to hear it – I value the sanity of my digestive tract even if you don't.' I watched with amusement as she slapped the cheese down, nibbling bits and licking her fingers as she tore off the plastic wrapping. The Stilton stood ready, nicely wrapped in a white napkin but an old piece of Cheddar joined the Camembert that we had bought that morning. 'Linkey!' I exclaimed. 'That cheese is all mouldy, you can't use that.'

'Doesn't matter, I'll just turn it over so the mouldy bit's underneath, it's good for you anyway, penicillin you know. The Sidis will be too polite to notice and the rest too blotto to care!' She stood back admiring her work.

'Well I shan't eat any I can tell you.'

'*Chacun à son gout*, and come on, I must go and check the fires.'

'If you don't need me for anything I think I'll go up and have a bath and change.'

'Of course, but I must say your poor body must be completely stripped of its natural oils with all this bathing, no wonder you feel the cold!' I gave her a friendly push and we laughed, happy in our friendship which passed far beyond the boundaries of our differing attitudes. 'Don't hurry, the Sidis will be the only people to arrive on time, the rest are always late.' I left her in the dining room heaping logs onto the fire.

When I reappeared Linkey had already changed and was sitting in her usual chair reading the paper. She looked astonishingly elegant and her hair was clean and organised, waving round her freshly made up face.

'You look great!' I exclaimed, knowing I sounded surprised.

'Thanks,' she said wryly, reading my thoughts. 'Did you think I would be wearing high heeled gumboots and a dog food bag? I can make an effort when I have to you know. Help yourself to a drink, it's all on the table by the piano.'

'Tell me about the rest of the guests.' I poured a glass of mineral water.

'Well, there's Tony and Anya Milligan. She's a Swede with a chequered career, one-time cabaret singer reputed to have had a string of aristocratic lovers before settling down with Tony. He's a dear and usually falls asleep but not till after the cheese. Then there's Val and Ian Wallace, he's nice too and she's great. Looks rather prim and severe but has a wicked sense of humour and a tendency to burst into song after a few jars. Bobby Loxley, he's the joke teller, and last but not least, Michael Stevens. He's small and clean and snuffles a lot so I thought he'd be ideal for you!'

I fell back into the sofa, amused by my friend's description of her guests. 'Oh Linkey, whatever are the poor Sidebottoms going to think of these people. I suppose they all smoke, drink, swear and chase innocent furry creatures?'

'Just about, yes! However, I consider it my civic duty to help them learn how to fraternise with the natives – it'll help them to integrate and enjoy life in the country.'

Suddenly, all the dogs jumped up and rushed out into the hall. 'That's them,' said Linkey, following the dogs out. As predicted, it was the time-conscious Sidebottoms.

The other guests arrived in dribs and drabs and we sat down to dinner at about 9 o'clock. From then on the evening passed in a blur of noise, smoke, merriment and people whose names I couldn't remember. Mrs Trouton produced a superb dinner and I even forgot to avoid the mouldy cheese. The Abbot family silver gleamed on the loaded table, glasses clinked, and Val Wallace treated us to *Dancing Queen.*

The Sidebottoms tried manfully to keep their end up, but it was obvious they were beginning to struggle as the evening gathered momentum. Everybody gave up trying to include them in the conversation except Linkey who, true to her self-imposed social conscience, continued to treat them with courtesy and interest. I knew they were aching to leave but lacked the courage to stand up and make their farewells. As I, too, was beginning to flag and the conversation had become local, I decided to help them out of their misery by making my excuses and saying goodnight.

I think Linkey understood for she made no objection when they followed my lead, and she escorted them to the hall, catching my eye and winking as she handed them their coats. I waited for them to leave, listening to the bursts of laughter that came from the dining room as Bobby the joke teller got under way.

'Thank you Rosie, do you really want to go to bed or where you just being kind?'

'I think I will go up actually if you don't mind. You were right about the sleepy Devon air, but it was a lovely evening and I wouldn't have missed it for the world. I think my next feature might well be called *Life Down Devon Way!*'

'I'm glad you enjoyed it, sleep well and see you in the morning.' Linkey gave a little wave and headed eagerly back to the party, like a hound that has scented its quarry.

I don't know what time the party finally broke up, but sounds of revelry continued to drift up to my room until I fell into a deep sleep and could only guess at what time Linkey finally came to bed.

The next day being Sunday, even Linkey had a lie-in and she was sitting in the kitchen drinking coffee when I came down. Mrs Trouton was beavering about and happily, few signs remained of the night before.

'Morning,' groaned Linkey, 'for heaven's sake don't shout or my head will fall off. Trust you to look all perky and clear of eye.' She groaned again, head in hands.

'Don't you be taking any notice of her, dear,' snapped Mrs Trouton, 'she was fine till you came in and if she isn't she's only one person to blame.'

'Oh shut up Trouty and don't call my friend *dear*, she's Miss Crossley to you.'

Mrs Trouton sniffed pointedly and left the room carrying a large tray loaded with clean silver. Linkey just laughed and threw a piece of toast at her retreating figure, much to the delight of the dogs who all rushed to gobble it up.

'Don't take any notice of all that, our strange banter is actually a sign of deep affection and respect. Dear old Trouty, long may she last, she is my prop and mainstay!' That I could well believe and I shuddered to think of what would become of the housekeeping at Wellshead if anything should happen to the old girl.

Linkey poured herself some more coffee and pushed the pot in my direction, smiling as she watched me brushing yet more dog hairs off my trousers.

'Poor old you!' she said, 'always so clean and neat, it must be awful for you to be surrounded by my filth! I really am sorry about the dog hairs though. Aunt Clarice Abbot bred deer hounds you know, that's why I've got them. The lurchers are what I really like but I felt obliged to carry on with these monsters as a sort of memorial to Aunt C. Being so huge, they don't live that long but they're all descended from one old bitch who was here long ago – isn't that so dears?' Linkey addressed the dogs who, knowing they were being discussed, stared at their mistress with devotion in their eyes, tails gently sweeping the floor better than any broom.

Sensing that Linkey was in a talkative mood, I helped myself to more coffee and hoped an opportunity would arise to ask about the locked room.

Being genuinely interested in antique furniture and objets d'art, I was hopeful that perhaps the room contained the treasures of Wellshead that were considered of sufficient value to be locked away. To spend a drab November Sunday morning looking at them would be a real treat.

Linkey lit up and stretched back in her chair. I would have to wait my moment.

'I love Sundays,' she announced. 'As long as all the

essentials are done, I never feel guilty being idle. One of the troubles with David was that he always had to be doing something useful and it ruined my relaxation time because it made me feel that I should be doing things too. What about you, what do you do most Sundays?'

'Oh, this and that – if I'm working then I keep working and if not, I catch up on the other things in life. You know, desk work, friends, house, all the usual stuff I suppose. But don't let's talk about that, tell me about this house, it's a fascinating old place.'

Linkey seemed happy to talk about the home which she clearly loved and told me the history of the house, its contents and the Abbots. Then, before the opportunity arose to ask about the locked room, a strange look crossed her face and she suddenly seemed to disappear from me.

'Come on, let's go down to the village and collect the papers then we can spend all afternoon in front of the fire reading the rubbish in all those ridiculous supplements.'

'Sounds good to me.' We crashed off down the lane on another terrifying, spine-jarring journey.

The day passed as those sort of days do, and it was not until early evening when Linkey was outside shutting up the chickens that I came across Mrs Trouton working in the kitchen.

'Don't you ever stop working, Mrs Trouton?' I asked, offering to help in case there was anything useful I could do. 'You sit down and have a cup of tea in peace and quiet before she gets back and starts her clattering.' she replied, ignoring my offer of help.

'Tell me,' I said casually as I sat down, 'why is the door upstairs on the small landing locked. Is the room full of lots of priceless treasures?'

I was completely unprepared for her response, which was as brief and sharp as the shatter of the glass that she dropped on the floor.

'That's nothing to do with nobody but Miss Lavinia and

don't you go asking her about it neither. Folks is best to mind their own business sometimes whoever they are.'

'I'm terribly sorry Mrs Trouton, I didn't mean to pry and I promise I'll never mention it again.' Her reaction shocked me, and I felt very uncomfortable and embarrassed.

'We'll just leave it like that then,' she said. 'Now come on and drink your tea and least said soonest mended.'

Linkey came back in a few minutes later, pink and damp from the rain that once more beat on the windows. We drank our tea together while The Old Trout continued to potter steadily about the kitchen, determined, I felt, to ensure that I did not continue with my curiosity.

'It really has been good to see you,' Linkey said between mouthfuls of tea, 'I can't tell you how much I've enjoyed having you. You will come again won't you?'

'Wild horses wouldn't stop me, particularly if I can see the debonair Mr Sidebottom again!'

We both laughed at the thought and one of the dogs got up and stuck its head on Linkey's lap, as if seeking reassurance that all was well in spite of our strange human noises. 'Poor Teasel,' she said, gently pulling its ears, 'there's nothing to worry about, it's only me and Aunt Rosie being silly.' The dog went and sat down and we finished our tea together.

I left Wellshead after breakfast the next day, and as I drove away down the lane, waving out of the car window, I saw them in my mirror standing in front of the old house, waving too: Linkey, Mrs Trouton and the dogs. What was their secret I wondered as they faded from view, and why was it so important that Linkey should never be asked about the locked room? *What does it matter*, I thought, mentally shrugging it off. People have secrets and I recalled someone once telling me that if a person had no secrets, they'd lived a very dull life. I was sure that would not apply to Linkey.

I had had a wonderful time and much looked forward to coming again, preferably in the summer when the house would be warm and dry and the countryside more appealing. Suddenly the thought of my own warm, dog-free home seemed very enticing, and as the miles of motorway sped by, Devon faded into another world, as remote and alien as the moon.

I turned into my street as daylight was beginning to fade and drew up with relief outside my front door. First stop tomorrow would definitely be the dry cleaners.

*

Time passed and Linkey and I remained in close contact. I went down to Devon from time to time and happily found nothing changed. I even managed to persuade Linkey to dig herself out and come and stay with me in London. Our friendship was as good as ever and I blessed the fates that had brought us together that day in the restaurant.

Not long after I had returned from a long week-end in Paris, I received a telephone call from Linkey telling me that Mrs Trouton had died suddenly in her sleep. She sounded distraught and although it was only mid-morning, I suspected that her sun had already gone well over the yardarm.

I said I would come down as soon as I could but I was leaving the next day for a short stay in Tanzania, where my nephew was getting married. There was no question of my cancelling the trip but I promised I would go down to Wellshead as soon as I returned. Linkey seemed overly dismayed by my news and I wondered what had become of her local friends who had been so happy to partake of her hospitality.

I was worried about my friend and as promised, as soon as I got back, I made my way down to Devon. Sadly my worries were well-founded, as when I reached Wellshead it was clear that Linkey had not recovered from Mrs Trouton's death. She looked ghastly and her drinking had become excessive. There were bottles of gin all over the house and although she never appeared drunk, I knew she was topping up more or less 24 hours of the day.

Of the dogs, only Mustard and Teasel remained and they alone were well-cared for and unchanged. The house was a complete tip. Dirty, chaotic and even colder than before. Linkey seemed to have given up on what she obviously considered to be a losing battle, and appeared to live entirely in the kitchen except for the few hours she spent in bed.

I stayed for a week and tried to help sort her out and I think in some measure succeeded, for when I left she seemed in much better spirits, and of a mind to make an effort to pull herself together. I asked about her friends but she just mumbled something about them being a dead loss. The unloved Sidebottoms, as Linkey had predicted, had been unable to stand the strain of country life and had bolted back to suburbia.

Our friendship continued much as before and as we both approached our 60th birthdays, which fell within weeks of one another, we planned a small celebration in London. Linkey said she would enjoy a visit which surprised me, as she had become even more rural in her old age. She had managed to find some help in the house and although nobody could ever replace The Old Trout, a nice woman from the village did what she could to look after things at Wellshead.

Linkey no longer enjoyed driving to London and I went to Paddington Station to meet her off the train. She stayed with me for three nights and we took ourselves to the theatre and visited various art galleries and museums. She particularly wanted to go to the Victoria & Albert to see Nelson's breeches. We couldn't believe how small he must have been, but she said that her father had told her that he was a tiny man, and now she had seen it for herself.

For her last night, we indulged in some real nostalgia and revisited the Kensington restaurant where we had met up again all those years ago. It had now become a trendy trattoria, staffed by dark, nimble waiters, who served us delicious pasta and Barolo in impeccable style. It was a wonderful evening that I shall never forget, and as the train pulled out of Paddington station the next day, Linkey waving madly, I hoped that she would come again. We had had such fun.

My next visit to Wellshead, some three months later, was a terrible shock. Linkey had deteriorated alarmingly and was drinking again, heavily. She appeared confused and distrait and was subject to violent mood swings. It was more than the exaggeration of personality traits that tends to come with old age and I felt powerless to help. She seemed as delighted to see me as ever, but after our initial greeting and settling in, she would disappear into a world that I could not penetrate. Where she went, I do not know, but try as I might, I could not follow.

On the day of my departure, she returned to normal and said how much she was looking forward to my next visit, and how I was the only real friend she had got left, apart from her one remaining dog, a grand-daughter of Slipper.

Linkey refused to come up to London, so I made the journey to Devon again through that summer to support my friend. I found it tiring and depressing and my visits, once so eagerly looked forward to, became times to dread and I found them stressful and sad. There seemed nothing I could do to help her and as, not surprisingly, she could no longer keep any staff, conditions at Wellshead had become untenable.

Eventually I could stand it no longer for the cold, the squalor and Linkey's behaviour were beyond my powers of endurance, and as I left Wellshead for what I knew would be the last time, my heart was heavy as I looked back on the good times we had shared together during our long friendship.

I never looked back that last time and as the station taxi bumped away down the lane, I preferred to remember that first visit. It was Linkey, Mrs. Trouton and the dogs, all standing together waving goodbye in front of a smiling, tidy Wellshead that I saw.

Linkey hung on for another six months, helped a little by her brother Victor. I knew she had left her entire estate to his daughter, Katherine, of whom she was very fond. I suspected his input to be motivated more by a desire to safeguard his daughter's inheritance than out of concern for his sister's welfare. Linkey and Katherine were soul mates, and I was pleased that there was at least one member of her family who genuinely cared about her.

*

Linkey died mercifully quickly of a heart attack. Apparently, had someone been with her at the time she might have been saved, but I knew that her spirit had long before left this world. I was thankful that she had not lingered but had gone as she would have wished, swiftly and without fuss.

Linkey left me a small 19th century water-colour which I had always admired, and a long letter, the contents of which shall remain private. I can only say that this letter is a possession that I cherish, an abiding testament to our friendship.

As I had begun to dislike long drives, I commandeered my neighbour's son, Mark, a charming university student who was always looking for pocket money, to drive me down to Devon for the funeral.

I had long ago shed my tears for my friend and as we ground our way through *The day Thou Gavest, Lord, has Ended*, I gazed around the small church, interested to see who else had turned out to honour Linkey in death.

Two pews in front of me stood an elderly but still upright man, and as he turned, like me surveying the small congregation, I knew immediately that it was David Maxwell. Age had withered him, like it does us all, but he was unmistakably the man on the piano and I resolved to speak to him when the service was over. There was to be a wake at Wellshead afterwards but I had no desire to go back to that house of memories and had told Mark that we would return to London directly the funeral service was over.

When it was all done and Linkey was finally laid to rest, I approached David Maxwell and introduced myself. He said that he too had no wish to go back to Wellshead but would like to speak to me, and suggested we go to a place he knew nearby where we could have a cup of tea in peace before going our separate ways. I liked him immediately and could only feel sad that Linkey had not remained married to this charming man.

It was during our conversation that I learned the secret of the locked room, and of that dark part of her that I had never been able to unearth. They had been married for just over two years, living happily at Wellshead, when Linkey had given birth to a son. They were both thrilled with the arrival of the baby and Linkey, in particular, had adored him. When he was three years old, he drowned in the lake at the end of the garden. Apparently she had never really recovered from the shock.

David told me how she had blamed herself for their child's death, as she had turned away for a brief moment, to pick some flowers, leaving him sitting near the lake playing with a toy car. When she turned round to check he was alright, he had disappeared. Rushing to the edge of the lake, she found him face-down in the water. All her efforts to resuscitate him were in vain. It was just one of those tragic accidents.

He was called Oliver and after his funeral, she had

piled all his small possessions into his room and locked the door. She threw the key into the lake and nobody had ever been into the room since. Their marriage had begun to break down soon after Oliver's death, when Linkey had started drinking heavily. David had tried everything to help her but finally she had told him that she wanted a divorce, for his presence was a constant reminder of her son and she could not rebuild her life while his father lived in the house. He had tried desperately to save their marriage but his efforts were in vain, and in the end they had parted and he had never seen her again.

I was stunned by what David told me and sat silent, staring into my tea cup. If only I had known, perhaps I could have helped, but it was all much too late now. No more pink gin and dog hairs, only memories, and who knew how much time left for me.

I stood up, and David helped me into my coat. I signalled to Mark, who had discreetly sat at another table and was being chatted up by the pretty young waitress.

David and I parted with a kiss and a smile and vows to keep in touch. But our season was gone and the days were drawing in. There would be no future for that part of my life – only a treasure trove of happy memories.

THE YEARS PASS...

BOOK FIVE: THE SINS OF THE FATHER

'Joey? It's Kate. Can you hear me, your phone's terrible!'

'Yeah, look I'll call you back, I'm on a bus. Give me twenty minutes.'

Joey Channon switched off her mobile and sat back in her seat to watch London go by. As the bus roared round Oxford Circus, she could still see signs of the debris left by the May Day demonstrations that had brought most of central London to a standstill.

The streets looked dirty and because it had been wet, some of the litter that had been trampled underfoot had stuck to the pavements. *Horrible job to clean that lot up*, she thought, flicking her long blond hair back as it flopped over her face, obscuring the dismal view.

'Sorry,' she smiled an apology at her neighbour, whose arm she had inadvertently jogged. But the pasty-faced woman barely acknowledged Joey's gesture and went on reading a tatty-looking magazine.

That was what the climate did for you she supposed, thinking about life back in Australia where she had been born and raised. She would never forget the Sydney Olympics which seemed to epitomise her life back home.

The fun, the excitement, the atmosphere and the acclaim of the world's press that had followed her country's efforts. No rioting or glum, pale faces there.

The bus reached Joey's stop and she jumped off, walking briskly along the few hundred yards it took her to reach the small restaurant where she worked as cook, bottle-washer, floor-sweeper or whatever else the man who owned it threw at her.

He was short, stout and Italian and his name was Attilio. He called her *cara mia Joeey* which made her giggle and want to kiss his walnut cheek. Joey liked him, and was quite happy to swing in with whatever was going. It suited her easy-breezy Australian attitude that went with the sunshine and freedom of her upbringing.

'Buon giorno Signor Attilio,' she pushed open the door. It amused her to greet him in his own language, even though her accent was atrocious.

'And to you too, cara mia Joeey. We are *veery, veery occupato* today so pleeze, *no loafin aroun* as you say.'

'Oh Mr. Attilio, *I mai, mai loaf aroun* - and it's *arounD* with a *D* anyway,' she laughed, striding through to the stuffy, dark little staff cloakroom to dump her coat.

Today was Joey's evening off, but the restaurant was fully booked for lunch and one of the boys who helped in the kitchen was off sick. They were all rushed off their feet from the word go, and she completely forgot her promise to telephone her friend Kate.

Joey was a healthy buxom girl, strong and energetic, but even she was tired by the time she returned home to the flat in Earls Court which she shared with an itinerant population of other young people.

As she dumped her clobber on the floor of the untidy little bedroom and threw herself onto the rumpled bed, she suddenly remembered Kate's call of the morning and reached for her mobile.

'Kate, hi it's me, Joey. I'm really sorry about not calling you back but work was manic. How's things?'

'Oh, OK I suppose though I'm pretty fed up with London and I think Henry and I are grinding to an unromantic halt.'

Henry was Kate's boyfriend of nearly a year whom Joey secretly thought rather boring. Typical upper-class pom was how she described him to herself. She hoped her friend would not be too upset.

'Sorry to hear that mate,' Joey answered dutifully. 'Did he do a *Daniel* or anything exciting like that?'

'What on earth's a *Daniel,* Joey?'

'You know, *Bridget Jones* and all that. When she and the luscious Hugh Grant, alias Daniel, were having a passionate bonking weekend in the hotel and he pretends...'

'Oh sorry, silly me,' laughed Kate, interrupting as the penny dropped. 'Good heavens no! Can you imagine dear old Henry doing anything so deliciously caddish! Actually I'm quite glad really, between you and me, it's all got rather boring. And it will annoy my aged parents who consider I'm on the shelf and thought Henry terribly suitable!'

'Know the feeling, old girl!'

'Anyway, the point is that for once the old things have had a sensible idea and have rented a house in France for three weeks in June. It sounds great and, can you believe it, Dad's said I can have the last week. Will you come?'

'Wild wallabies wouldn't stop me; I can't wait to get out of London. Sounds brilliant Kate and thanks for asking me, I'd love to come.'

'Look, I've got to dash but let's meet up after the week-end and get the French job properly organised. It sounds like we could have some fun. I'll ring you – bye for now.'

Joey dropped her phone on the floor and lay back on the bed, stretching her arms above her head. The idea of the French holiday with Kate suddenly lifted the gloom she had begun to feel after a winter in London.

It would be a good opportunity to see a bit of Europe, too, and when the Northern Hemisphere summer was over, she would head home. A wave of homesickness washed over her as she thought about her parents and brothers back home on their sheep station in New South Wales.

Wish I could ring them, she thought, *no point – they'll all be asleep.* She would tell Attilio about her plans tomorrow, and as her mind wandered off she fell asleep.

*

Time sped past, and Joey worked all the hours she could to save as much money as possible for the French holiday. She was also making a great effort to lose weight, and had taken up running as part of her campaign to reinvent her bikini figure which had spread alarmingly during the winter after a diet of pasta and coke. Flabby white flesh was not on her holiday agenda. Luckily she tanned easily as her Australian skin was used to the sun, and she made the most of the early summer rays which at last began to spread over London.

Joey was jogging back to her flat one morning after her run, and had just arrived at the bottom of the steps that led up to the front door, when she noticed a tall youth scrutinising the phalanx of buzzer buttons identifying the individual flats in the building.

'Hi!' she panted, her face red and sweaty. His pleasant face looked anxious and his thick, wavy brown hair dishevelled, but his overall appearance was clean and normal. *No psycho rapist here.* Joey wondered who he was looking for.

'Hello,' he replied, smiling vaguely. 'I'm looking for Jemma Phillips. I think she lives in Flat 11 but I've lost the bit of paper with all her details on it.'

'That's my flat too as luck would have it, but Jemma's away at the moment. She's gone to Cornwall for a week.'

'Oh no, that's a nuisance,' he replied sounding genuinely distressed. 'What on earth shall I do now,' he muttered to himself.

'Look, you'd better come in,' said Joey, taking pity on him. 'I'm sure your problem can't be that serious,' and she opened the door and led the way up to Flat 11.

'Find a space if you can and I'll brew some coffee. Sorry about the mess but some of the others had a party last night - I'm Joey by the way.'

'I'm Ben Cardew and thank you for rescuing me, I appreciate it.'

Ben stared round the chaotic sitting room, looking for somewhere to sit that was free from the debris of last night's revelry. Dirty glasses and overflowing ashtrays covered every surface, and the floor was littered with empty bottles and some worryingly intimate articles of female clothing.

Joey returned with two mugs of coffee and flopped down in a tatty arm chair, squashing several empty CD covers that were hidden under a cushion.

'Boy, I'm knackered! I'm trying to lose weight for my hol in June but all this running is wearing me out. Anyway, what's your story, how do you know Jemma?'

'I don't really, but she's a friend of my sister and the only person we know in London who might have been able to put me up for a couple of nights while I sort something out.'

'So what's the big problem?' asked Joey, still unable to understand why Ben seemed so bothered.

'I can't go home, that's the problem. My father's a dairy farmer and there's been an outbreak of Foot & Mouth on the next door farm. We have a suspected case now too and the entire herd will be slaughtered. It's an absolute disaster.'

'Oh Ben, how awful. My folks farm in Australia and it would kill Dad if something like that happened, I'm really sorry. Can't you go back though? I should think your family could use some support right now.'

'I wish I could, I've just spoken to Mum and she's in tears but once you've got an A notice slapped on, your property is cordoned off and that's it. Once all the cows have been killed and burnt and everything disinfected, I might be able to go back, but with MAFF being so useless, God knows when that will be.'

'Look Ben, I've got to go to work, I'm late already but if it's any help you can stay here for a couple of nights. The flat's not exactly *The Ritz* but if you can stand the squalor, you're welcome. I know Jemma wouldn't mind you using her room.'

'Honestly Joey, that's very kind of you, I don't know what to say.'

'Well say *yes* then, dumb head!' Joey answered with her Australian candour.

'All right then, I will. But only on condition that you let me take you out to supper tonight.'

'Can't do tonight, I'm working, but tomorrow will do just as well. Here look, you had better have my key and tell any of the tramps who live in this dump who you are when they turn up.' A look of alarm crossed Ben's face at the mention of the other inmates. 'Don't worry,' Joey laughed, 'they won't eat you though they might try to tear your clothes off! Must dash – see you later.'

Joey rushed off, leaving Ben to contemplate his situation. He heard the front door slam and looking out of the dirty window, watched her running down the road to catch a bus which miraculously arrived at just the right moment. As the bus and Joey disappeared down the street, he turned away and pondered on his next move. He felt depressed and all at sea. He quite enjoyed visiting London from time to time but he was a countryman at heart, and to be stuck in a city against his wishes was not an experience he relished.

Ben's mother had brought her children up to make the best of any situation that life threw at them, and she had no time for moping. She had successfully stamped her attitude into her son's subconscious, and as he looked at the mess that was Flat 11, he decided to tidy it up. Not only would the task give him something positive to do but it would also, he presumed, smooth the daunting path of his introduction to the returning inhabitants of the flat. The traditional concept of males being the mess-makers and females the domestics had long gone by the board, and in Ben's limited experience, the opposite often applied.

An hour and a half later the room was unrecognisable and Ben decided to pat himself on the back by going out to lunch, followed by a visit to the cinema to see *Captain Corelli's Mandolin*. The film was all the rage, and it was almost impossible to read a newspaper without some reference to it appearing in print. Ben had struggled through the 435 pages of the paperback, skipping chunks along the way, and he hoped that Pelagia in the shape of Penelope Cruz might prove to be more alluring than the Pelagia of the endless pages. He imagined it would probably be the type of film his mother would enjoy, and he would like to have been able to ring her and say *Jump on a train, meet me and we'll go together* but of course, his parents would not be able to go anywhere for some weeks.

Thank goodness he had not been at home when the outbreak was confirmed or he, too, would have been stuck and his job as a milking machine engineer put in jeopardy.

The cinema was full, and as he squeezed apologetically along a row of seated people, Ben chuckled inside at his situation. A lone man at a matinee – they probably all thought he was some sort of frustrated pervert. As he folded his gangly body into the only available seat, he smiled at his left-hand neighbour who supported his theory by glaring back before edging away and resuming her popcorn munching.

Ben enjoyed the film on a medium level. He was neither engrossed nor deeply moved, and by the time it ended his long legs were cramped and longing to stretch. He had not dared shift them around during the showing in case his wary neighbours thought he was making some strange sexual overture. His visit to the cinema had filled the empty afternoon, but as he shuffled out with the crowd, back into the busy streets of London, he began to worry again about his immediate future.

It was kind of the girl, Joey, to say he could camp down in the flat for a day or two and he would have to make the best of it. Hotels in London were expensive and he would rather muddle through in Flat 11 than spend the sort of money required on some cheap, drab hotel even supposing he could find a room at such short notice.

The flat was empty when he returned, but the other occupants began to arrive back in dribs and drabs shortly after he had made himself a cup of tea. The milk floated in nasty little globules on the top, and as he chucked it down the sink, he heard the door open and braced himself against the coming onslaught.

However, his worries were unfounded and the girls accepted Ben without surprise or question. People come and go here all the time, they said with friendly smiles, and if it really had been him who had cleared up after the party, he was welcome any time.

Ben hardly saw Joey, who arrived back late and left early again the next morning, but they made a plan to meet at Attilio's restaurant that evening for Ben's promised dinner.

As a member of staff, Joey and one friend could eat for nothing once a month, provided they paid for any drink and ate the cheapest set menu. They also had to sit down early, and be finished and gone before the main evening rush started between 8.30 and 9.

'Here's the address, don't lose it,' Joey said, 'I'll see you later.'

Ben enjoyed his dinner with Joey. He liked the frankness of the Australian girl and her uncomplicated optimistic attitude to life. She made him laugh and he was sorry when Attilio, fat stomach encased in a long white apron, marched up to their table and turned them out.

'Cara mia Joeey – it ees time you go and take your *amante* with you,'and he smiled his spaghetti smile and touched Joey lightly on the shoulder.

'He's not my *amante* but we've had real fun and thanks for giving us the bottle of wine – I shall work extra hard tomorrow!' and they all laughed as Attilio rolled his near-black eyes towards the ceiling.

'Yes,' agreed Ben, 'thank you very much, it was all delicious and I shall definitely go for Italian wine in future.'

They walked out of the restaurant into a fine, warm evening, and neither of them felt like going back to the stuffy, impersonal flat.

'Let's go to a place I know in the park where we can sit outside and get a drink, or coffee or ice cream if you want,' suggested Joey.

'That sounds great. I'm not a city man I'm afraid and with the weather like this, I've a yearning to be outdoors and preferably in sight of something green.'

'Me too, in fact I can't wait to get out of London. I'm really lucky as a mate of mine has asked me to go to France with her next month. Come on, here's the bus.'

They jumped on and within a short time were seated at an outside table with a pot of coffee and two large ice creams. The air was warm but fresh, and the grass in the park still the clean, brilliant green of early summer. Suddenly the population looked happy, as if the sunshine were a magical panacea for the ills of winter.

Knowing the English, the time would soon come when they would all be complaining it was too hot, thought Joey as she sat watching Ben pour the coffee.

'Black for me and no sugar, thanks,' she said, taking the cup. 'So, have you got anything sorted out yet?'

'More or less, I think. I've fixed up to lodge with a chap who works for the same company as me and luckily, I left my car at the station instead of getting a lift in with Mum. It would have been a major bore if my car had been impounded as I've left lots of vital work stuff in it.'

'Don't you find it a bit restricting living at home at your age?'

'Not really, and I'm away a lot of the time anyway. I suppose I rather like having home comforts without the hassle and expense of having to run my own place. Also, I can help out with the milking when I'm not away which gives my father a break. Not that we shall have that problem now,' he finished bitterly.

'Have you spoken to your parents today?'

'Yes, I rang this afternoon and spoke to Dad. All the cows have been slaughtered but they're still lying in a heap in the yard. It's very near the house so it's pretty unpleasant and nobody seems to know when the carcasses will be shifted. They've rushed off to slaughter everything in the contiguous zone regardless of whether the cattle have the disease or not.'

'What on earth does contiguous mean?'

'It's what any normal person would call next-door or adjoining or adjacent, take your pick. Why on earth they have to come up with some word most farmers have to look up in the dictionary when an ordinary one would do, God knows. It's typical of MAFF and this government.'

'What does MAFF stand for anyway?'

'Multiply Admin and Fuck the Farmers!' answered Ben, laughing. 'Actually it stands for Ministry of Agriculture, Fisheries and Food.'

'Oh dear!' Joey laughed too, 'you poor poms have a terrible time of it – you should come to Oz.'

'In fact I'd love to, Australia's a country I've always wanted to visit, but somehow I never got round to going. I suppose I'm not very adventurous by nature and now I'm stuck in my job. What brought you over here?'

'I always wanted to travel and most of us Aussies still have a desire to see little old England and Europe too. In fact, my mother's English, so in my case I have a particular reason for wanting to come here.'

'Oh I see,' said Ben, sounding surprised. 'Have you got family over here then?'

'Only an uncle who lives in the West Country. He's Mum's younger brother but they were never very close. She calls him an uncommunicative old misery guts! Apparently he had some big love trouble when he was young and went a bit odd and disappeared abroad. Then he had a bad skiing accident that left him semi-crippled.'

'Sounds great! Have you been to see him or has he locked himself away from the world?'

'Yes and no. I mean yes, I have been to see him and no, he's not some weird and terrifying recluse. In fact, to my astonishment he seemed very pleased to see me and was rather kind and fun. I rang Mum to tell her and she asked if I was sure I was staying with the right person!'

'Perhaps he's terribly rich and will leave you all his money!' laughed Ben.

'Sadly I don't think he's particularly rich and he got married late in life to a woman who lived next door to the place he was renting – all rather romantic really. No kids though, so you never know your luck!'

'Maybe marriage has improved him.'

'Could have I suppose, my new aunt's really nice. She's called Isobelle and I'm going to see them again before I go home. I think they both expected a sort of female Crocodile Dundee waving a boomerang, but when I turned out to be a normal human being, they seemed chuffed that I'd showed up. They were so happy together it would have been impossible not to have enjoyed being with them and they had this nice old lady called Martha who did most of the work, which made it even better! What about you, you've mentioned your parents but have you got brothers or sisters, or are you a lonely only?

'I've got a sister called Lucy – she's a bit older than me and we used to spar a bit as kids – usual sort of stuff you know - but now we get on really well. She had a bad riding accident when she was young and was in a coma for ages. Poor Mum nearly went mad.'

'Gosh I'm not surprised – how awful. What happened?'

'It's a long story but she's fine now, just a bit vague sometimes.' Ben looked at his watch. 'Come on Joey, I think we'd better go. I must be away early tomorrow and you've got all that extra work to do to pay for our wine!'

'It was my pleasure Ben boy, and I think your little London stay has done you good.'

'Thanks to you for putting up with me! How long will it take to walk back to the flat?'

'Too long and I've got a much better idea – let's go for broke and get a taxi. It won't be too bad if we share.'

'Sounds sense to me – let's go get one.'

Early the next morning, Ben crept out of Flat 11 and away back to his troubled life. He was due some holiday in June and was looking forward to a break. He would have to see what the situation was like at home before deciding what he would do with his precious time off.

Joey left the flat sometime later and as the bus trundled along, she too thought how much she was looking forward to her holiday. She had had enough of London, and the money she had saved would be enough to get her through the rest of her time in England without having to work anymore.

Only a short time left now before she would be en route to France. *I must ring Kate,* she thought, *I can't wait to make our plans and discuss an idea with her.*

*

'Don't tell me, old cobber, that you've fallen in love with a pom!' shrieked Kate when Joey told her about Ben, as the two friends were sitting in Kate's flat discussing the French trip over supper.

'Don't be daft and don't call me *cobber*.'

Kate could never resist an opportunity for *Aussie-speak,* as she called it, knowing perfectly well that Joey did not mind in the least, and often aped an exaggerated English accent in return.

'Ben's not that sort of bloke,' continued Joey.

'Oh! I hope he's not weird or anything, if that's what you mean,' interrupted Kate, 'it's bad enough taking a kangaroo!'

'And what's that supposed to mean, dear friend?'

'Well, I told my mother you were known as *The Kangaroo* because you suffered from a rare disorder of the legs and could only hop.'

'Thanks a bunch, and what did your mother say?'

'*Don't be so stupid, Katherine. No wonder you've failed to find a husband.*' That's her stock remark when addressing her daughter.'

'I'm not surprised,' Joey laughed, 'now if I may continue, what I mean is that Ben is a normal male but rather shy and unworldly about life. I liked him and felt a bit sorry for him and thought it would be nice if he came too. Quite useful to have a male along in case we have a puncture or something like that. And he's ace at washing up! We're not an item, he's just a friend who happens to be a member of the opposite sex', she added, wondering if perhaps Kate might be worried about feeling spare.

'If he wants to come, I don't have any objections - the house has 4 double bedrooms so there's plenty of room. He'll have to spend the first night on the floor or somewhere though, as we overlap with the parents for one night and they've got friends with them.'

'Ben won't mind that – if he can survive two nights at my flat, he can survive anything.'

'Fancy a lager?' Kate stretched her arms above her head. 'Hmm, I can't wait to be beside the swimming pool with nothing to do but laze.'

'Me too,' agreed Joey, getting up to fetch two cans from the kitchen, knowing that Kate's offer meant she would like one herself but couldn't be bothered to get it.

Her cooking was haphazard to put it mildly, and as Joey studied the disarray in the kitchen, she wondered how much time she would have to spend tidying up behind her friend in France.

'I've had another thought,' she said as she came back with the drinks, 'Ben's brilliant at washing up. He cleared up the flat after the tramps' party the other night.'

'Great,' cried Kate, 'I'm useless at all that as you know! We won't have to bother too much though, that's the beauty of country France. Life's so easy, we can eat out for next to nothing, or buy all that wonderful food in the markets and live off cheese, pâté, salad, oysters, fruit – you name it. Eating's not a drag like it is in England.'

'Lucky I've lost nearly a stone then or I should end up looking like a whale,' said Joey, sighing enviously as she looked at her tall, skinny friend. 'It's all right for you, you don't have to worry.'

'True, but then everything levels out. You don't have to put up with frizzy hair, stubby eyelashes and a giant hooter,' retorted Kate.

'Oh come on Kate, I'd much rather have your distinctive nose than the squashed pickled onion I've got stuck in the middle of my face, and on the rare occasions when you bother with your hair, it looks great.'

'Ugh, you're beginning to sound like my mother! Which reminds me, when we arrive we will be given endless instructions about how to look after the house, what we must and must not do and so forth, but we just smile and say yes and take no notice.'

'I get the idea, though I don't believe your parents are half as bad as you make out,' answered Joey.

'Oh, they're OK. Of course I love them really, but they do treat me like an imbecile which irritates me, as you can imagine. Their friends, Sam and Dotty Renshaw are quite jolly, you'll like them. The four of them play golf all day and bridge all night which is seriously boring but it keeps them happy.'

'Where is this house anyway? You haven't told me a thing about it – maybe your folks have got a point about the imbecile bit!'

'Oh ha ha! Would you like me to show you where France is on the map of the world? I suppose you know the joke about the difference between an Aussie and yoghurt?'

'Aw! Not that again – *yoghurt's got a live culture,'* sighed Joey.

'The house is in Gascony, in the south-west. We've got a long drive ahead but that's all part of the holiday. If we steer clear of the auto routes, which are boring and expensive, we can see more of the country and maybe spend a night on the Loire and look at a château or two.'

'Sounds great,' enthused Joey, 'I'd really like to do that. Mum's always banging on about the Loire, I think she went there to learn French when she was young. Can you speak French by the way? I can't speak a word.'

'Enough to get by and a bit more. Don't worry, you'll soon pick up the basics and that's all you need. Lots of the Frogs speak a bit of English - they're much better at languages than we tend to be.'

'Only two more weeks of sweat and toil! I don't think I have ever looked forward to a holiday so much.' Joey smiled at the thought.

'I know,' agreed Kate. 'It's been a rubbish winter and what with sacking Henry it really will be nice to get away. Tell you what, I've got a book somewhere that tells you all about Gascony. I'll dig it out and then you can study it before we go. Knowing a bit about the area makes it all the more interesting and as we've only got a week, we might as well make the most of it.'

'Thanks, I'd like that. But now I'd better be going. I have to be early at work tomorrow, we've got some special lunch party booked and the boy who helps in the kitchen is still off sick.'

Kate yawned as her friend stood up. 'I'm whacked too, I didn't get to bed till 2.30 this morning and I'm getting too old for too much booze and too little sleep!'

'I'll ring you when I've spoken to Ben and see you soon. Thanks for supper.'

The door slammed and Kate looked round the untidy room and the mess in the kitchen. The large, smart flat belonged to her parents, but they seldom used it and never without prior warning. She decided the tidying up operation could wait until the morning, and went to find the book on Gascony before she forgot her promise to Joey.

She liked the Australian girl and hoped that their friendship had contributed to her enjoyment of her time in England, and that it would continue after Joey had returned home. Maybe one day Kate might take a trip to the other end of the world.

Ben was astonished and delighted to receive Joey's invitation to join the two girls on the Gascon venture. He wondered if they really wanted him to come, but Joey had been insistent and it had taken little persuasion for him to accept.

He was bored with his job, depressed about the situation at home in particular, and farming in general, and worried about his future. What could be a better tonic than sun, fun and a change of scene? Perhaps it would help him to sort out his life and decide which way he was going.

Now he had made the decision to go, he counted off the days till the holiday, like he had once done as a school boy, waiting for term to end.

Joey bid a fond farewell to Mr Attilio, who gathered together the small staff of his restaurant to give a farewell party in her honour. The little Italian drank rather too much Chianti Classico and became sentimental. Still wearing his famous apron and brandishing a large, bolognaise-covered spoon, he burst into *E lucevan le stelle* from Tosca, two large tears appearing in his luminous eyes. They all succumbed to the atmosphere created by the boss, and drank and laughed until it was time to go. Everyone kissed, and a short chapter in Joey's life ended. Time to move on to the next stop - *La Belle Gascogne.*

*

'Au revoir Agen,' sang Kate as they whizzed over the Garonne and headed south. 'You won't suffer from constipation if you live here – their speciality is prunes!'

'Thanks for the info,' said Joey before turning to speak to Ben, who was sharing the back seat of Kate's car with a mountain of plastic bags and a bursting rucksack.

'You OK there Ben?' she asked. 'Or would you like to change places and take over the navigation?'

'I'm fine thanks, and you're better at map reading than me anyway.'

Joey smiled and turned back to the route plan that Kate had written out before they left England.

'Hey, get this chaps, the next stop's called Condom!' and they all giggled stupidly as the holiday spirit rendered them infantile. Even Ben had at last lost his shyness, and joined with the other two as they chattered and joked their way through France.

'It's pronounced *c'ndom* with a stress on the *dom* bit, not Condom and do you know, it's the most photographed town sign in Europe – by the English that is,' said Kate in a superior tone of voice.

'Oh do let's stop and take a photo,' cried Joey, 'my folks would just love a pic of me leaning on a French letter!'

'OK I'll take one of you two, and as we've got heaps of time, let's stop for a cold beer or an *orange pressé*, I'm parched,' agreed Kate.

'Bon idée,' replied Joey, who had been trying to learn

some basic French and was rather proud of her progress.

The famous photograph taken, they drew up in the town square and were soon seated outside a café, cold drinks on the table.

Kate stretched her legs out and took a long swallow, wiping the froth off her mouth with the back of her hand.

'Hmm, that tasted good,' she said, putting the glass down and lighting a cigarette. 'We've only got about half an hour's drive left I reckon, and I told the parents we would arrive about 6, so we can take our time. Why don't you drive the last leg Ben?' she suggested, feeling it might help his self-confidence if he arrived at the wheel, rather than falling out of the back under a pile of luggage.' Joey silently thanked her friend for her perception. She felt responsible for Ben's enjoyment of his holiday as it had been at her instigation that he had joined them.

Sensing his hesitation, Kate continued: 'I wouldn't mind a break from driving and it would give me time to compose myself before *l'arrival*!'

'Sure, no problem,' he agreed, and ordered another round of drinks, secretly pleased that Kate had asked him.

'Left – no, straight on – where's the damn wheely-bin?' Kate shouted endless confusing directions from the back seat. 'We've got to turn left at a big wheely-bin, then first right 200 yards later opposite a sign saying Armagnac *vente direct*.'

Poor Ben drove slowly on, with no option but to do as he was instructed. Kate had been confident that her father's directions would lead them with ease to Le Rouchinon, which was the name of the house they had rented.

Joey was too busy exclaiming at the beautiful vineyards that they passed to take much notice of driver and navigator, but after several wrong turns, Kate at last spotted the desired landmark.

'Here we are - this must be it. Turn left Ben and go

slow.'

Ben did as he was commanded and sure enough, on the right after a couple of hundred yards, two stone pillars came into view. A scruffy home-made notice, slightly askew, proclaimed Le Rouchinon, and underneath it was a *Gîtes de France* sign.

'Hurrah, we've made it!' The girls exclaimed, as Ben drove slowly up the long, sandy-coloured drive with a green middle of grass and weeds.

They could see chimneys and a glimpse of a terracotta coloured roof, and as they rounded a bend at the top, an old Gascon *manoir* came into view. The grass in front of the house looked wispy and parched, and was dotted with little box trees. Beyond it, shimmering quietly in the early evening sun, lay a large blue swimming pool. An L-shaped range of wisteria covered outbuildings formed a courtyard, where two smart cars were parked.

'Oh Kate!' gasped Joey, 'what a lovely old place.'

'Looks good, doesn't it?' she agreed. 'Hoot the horn Ben, let's alert the reception committee.'

Ben beeped politely on the horn, and as the car came to a halt, a man and a woman appeared from round the side of the house, smiling and waving.

Kate jumped out and went to greet her parents, whom she kissed affectionately before turning to introduce her friends.

'Joey Channon, Ben Cardew. Meet my mother and father.'

'Victor and Audrey Amberly,' said the man, stepping forward and shaking hands. 'We are delighted to see you all and welcome to Le Rouchinon.'

Kate had inherited her mother's head on her father's body, and was unmistakably their daughter. But whereas Audrey Amberly was immaculately groomed from top to toe, Kate seldom bothered a jot about her appearance, and it was easy to see why mother and daughter might lack a depth of understanding.

'Come and meet Sam and Dotty and then we'll get you unpacked and organised,' said Audrey. 'It's Christian names all round by the way.'

Half an hour later, luggage in and rooms sorted, the three sticky travellers were relaxing in the swimming pool, washing away the stains of the journey.

'Come and join us when you are ready,' said Audrey from the pool side, 'there's a terrace round the other end that gets the evening sun and your father's got some champagne on ice, so hurry up if you want some.'

Kate raised a hand in acknowledgement of her mother's offer and duck dived down to the bottom of the pool, surfacing again seconds later, water streaming off her plastered hair.

'This is the life,' she spluttered, 'I'm off to the champagne bar!'

'How tidy should we be?' asked Joey who had noticed the chic casuals of the two older women.

'Oh wear any old thing, whatever's most comfortable. And Ben, get some shorts on, those lanky legs of yours are even whiter than mine!'

'I think I shall wait till tomorrow if you don't mind,' laughed Ben, 'I'm not ready for exposure yet!'

By the time Joey and Ben joined the others, Kate was already seated and sipping champagne. Her untouched hair was still dripping onto an old white T-shirt, and she had a towel round her waist and bare feet. A mild argument was already in progress between mother and daughter.

'Really darling,' Audrey was saying, 'I know we're on holiday but you could make a little more effort with your appearance. And please put those disgusting cigarettes away, you know I cannot abide you smoking.'

'Oh don't nag Mummy. Sam smokes and you don't seem to object to that.' And she winked at Sam, who was round, red and jolly with crinkly little blue eyes that were always smiling.

'Sam's not my daughter,' snapped Audrey.

'Gosh Mummy, and here's me thinking he was my sister!' countered Kate, laughing.

'Now stop it you two,' chipped in Victor. 'Let's call a truce and enjoy our short stay together. Your mother's right, Kate, replace that towel with some form of normal garment and bring some olives and nuts from the kitchen on your way back.'

Kate flounced off, and her mother took a deep breath through her nose and a large swallow of champagne.

'Sorry Vic darling, and I know I shouldn't speak ill of the dead, but Katherine is becoming alarmingly like your sister Lavinia, and it worries me.'

'*Don't* worry, my dear,' Victor replied, patting his wife's knee, 'Kate's got enough of your genes to keep her feet on the ground.'

The Renshaws smiled, and Dotty turned to Joey and Ben who had sat down, looking brushed and tidy but somewhat ill at ease.

'*Santé*!' she smiled, raising her glass to them, 'and welcome to Gascony.'

The bubbles in the recently poured wine fizzed up the glass where they snapped and foamed on the surface of the pale gold liquid, reminding Joey of their consumer. Dotty was all bubble and sparkle but instead of being pale gold and chilled, she was dark and warm and Joey liked her on sight.

'Tell me about yourself, Ben,' Dotty invited. 'I gather your poor family has been hit by this wretched Foot & Mouth disease. How terrible for you all.'

'Yes, it is a blow, particularly for my father who inherited our herd from my grandfather. It takes years to build up a good dairy herd and we still had the original female line. Now it's all gone in a few hours. Dad doesn't know what to do with himself and the compensation for the slaughtered stock is nothing compared to the total destruction of a way of life he has known since childhood. Also, of course, they have no income now.'

'We've read such awful things about it in the papers,' joined in Sam, 'how carcasses are left for days, rotting under the farmers' noses before being disposed of. Is that true?'

'I'm afraid it is,' replied Ben. 'MAFF simply can't cope and it's very distressing for people like my parents. You see, to them the cows are individuals, with different characteristics and personalities. My father knew every one of his cows and most had names. I don't think non-farming people understand how attached a stockman like Dad becomes to his animals and what they mean to him.'

'Will he start again do you think?' asked Dotty.

'I honestly don't know,' said Ben, frowning at the question. 'I suppose if I wanted to take on the farm, he probably would, but I'm not sure that I do. I don't have the feel for stock that he has, and you have to be totally committed to be a good dairy farmer. Also, the future of farming in England is very uncertain at the moment.'

'Have you got brothers and sisters?' asked Sam.

'I've one sister, Lucy, she's married with a baby and her husband's got his own farm, mostly cereals and a few sheep.'

At that moment Kate reappeared, carrying a tray full of bowls of green olives, crisps and nuts. Ben was relieved, for although he appreciated the Renshaw's kindness in drawing him into the conversation, he wanted to push England to the back of his mind for the duration of his short holiday.

The truce between mother and daughter was kept, and a tidy, fagless Kate smiled at her mother as she sat down. There was no more nagging, or reference to the infamous Aunt Lavinia, and the seven contented people relaxed and talked together, in harmony with the Gascon countryside which surrounded them.

Immaculate vineyards stretched away, merging into small rolling hills, dotted with russet roofed farmsteads. In the far distance, the highest tips of the Pyrenees could just be seen reaching up to the sky.

The land of Armagnac and of D'Artagnan, as Victor Amberly pointed out as they rose to go inside for supper, scattering the small lizards who had crept out onto the edge of the terrace to catch the last rays of the sun.

Kate had been right, and after breakfast the next morning, their remaining time together with the Amberlys was taken up with endless instructions about the care of the house.

Dotty and Sam had bolted to the nearby golf course for a last nine holes, and after an early lunch, the four oldies piled into their smart cars and with much kissing and waving, disappeared down the drive in a cloud of dust.

Kate had tolerated her parents' drilling with patience and good humour and much to the relief of her friends, there had been no further arguments with her mother.

As the sound of the cars died away and the dust settled behind them, Kate let out a loud *yippee,* and threw the list of instructions her mother had given her into the bin.

'Now we can get on with our holiday,' she announced. 'Let's finish the wine and have a committee meeting to decide what we all want to do.

'Do tell us, Kate,' said Joey when they were all sitting down again, 'who was the dreaded Aunt Lavinia your mother seemed so *un* fond of?'

'She was my father's younger sister and I adored her. She was always called Linkey, and was the best fun and so laid back about life. Needless to say, my parents strongly disapproved of her. Sadly, she drank herself to death *much* too young – it was horrible actually.'

'That's so sad,' said Joey. Fun relations are hard to

come by.'

'I know, I still miss her a lot. She had this fabulous old house in Devon, all dogs and disorder – just the sort of place I love. Actually, she left everything to me, but I can't get my hands on it till I'm 30 – some weird trust fund or something.'

'Wow - lucky old you!' exclaimed Joey.

'Why did she never get married?' asked Ben.

'She did, and she had a son called Oliver. But when he was very small, he drowned in the lake at Wellshead – that's her house. It was a terrible tragedy and according to Dad, she went a bit potty after it happened, and her marriage broke up not long after.'

'What a dreadfully sad story,' said Ben. 'So what's happened to the house now?'

'It's let at the moment, but all the rent goes towards paying off the huge amount it cost to modernise it. I don't benefit at all yet, but I'm jolly well going to live there one day though, *somehow*.'

'Funny that,' said Joey, 'I've got a long lost uncle who lives in Devon too, on the edge of Exmoor. He had some unfortunate affair and went a bit potty apparently, though he's fine now. Do you think we've both got dodgy genes in our makeup?'

'Highly likely I should think,' laughed Kate, 'but who cares!'

'I remember you telling me about your uncle,' said Ben. 'You two seem to have very exciting families compared to me – no black sheep or skeletons in the Cardew cupboard I'm afraid.'

'Well, I'm glad you haven't got any sheep in your cupboards, black or white,' said Kate. 'But tell us about your sister, do you get on well together?'

'Yes we do, I'm pleased to say. Lucy's three years older than me, but we got on pretty well as children most of the time. She had a bad riding accident when she was 13 which left her with funny vision and dizzy spells for ages afterwards, but she's fine now and very happy with her husband and baby. That reminds me, I promised to send them a post card, so don't let me forget.'

'We'll have to shop tomorrow anyway, so we can do all that kind of thing at the same time,' said Kate. 'Dotty said there's a good cheap and cheerful restaurant about three miles from here which I suggest we pay a visit to this evening.'

'Sounds OK by me,' said Joey, and Ben nodded in agreement.

The first afternoon was spent swimming, sun-bathing and sleeping by the two girls, but Ben decided to go for a walk and explore the surrounding country. He enjoyed bird-watching and set off with a pair of binoculars and a pocket bird book.

The paraphernalia of summer holidays soon littered the hitherto tidy house, and paperbacks, sun cream and dark glasses were strewn round the pool side.

'It's terribly exhausting doing nothing,' muttered Kate from under her large straw hat.

'Hmm,' agreed Joey, 'but it's a kind of exhaustion I can live with.'

She was floating in the pool, face down on a lilo and thinking about nothing but the perfect clarity of the water beneath her. How different this tame water was to the awesome power of the sea back home. She rolled off the lilo and flopped in the water, luxuriating in its coolness. Soon the afternoon was gone.

Dotty's restaurant was exactly the sort of place they hoped it would be. The village was an ancient hilltop Bastide, unspoilt by the passage of time, and the restaurant itself was situated under the old arches, the outside tables covered with white paper cloths. Baskets of geraniums hung from the walls, the brilliant red of the flowers contrasting perfectly with the old grey stone. A hand-written board propped up outside proclaimed *menu de jour - petit pichet et service compris.*

'This looks great,' said Joey as they wished the owner *bonsoir* and settled at a table. Ben enthused about his walk, and in particular about the acres of vines that he had seen.

'Do you think we could look round a wine place?' he asked Kate, 'or are they all very private. I'd love to see what goes on and learn a bit about wine making and the local wines.'

'Yeah, good idea,' Joey agreed, 'I'd like that too. We can't waste the whole week doing nothing but eat and laze and I'd like to see one of those goose farms too, where they stuff them with maize for foie gras'.

'I don't know about that,' replied Kate, 'but I'm sure we could visit a wine place if we knew who to ask. We'll try and find out tomorrow when we go into town.'

The food arrived and they fell to eating with gusto. Every course was delicious; simple but fresh, tasty and nicely presented.

'If only we could eat like this for about six quid at home,' said Kate, forking slim, crispy *pommes frites* into her mouth. 'Compare these to that soggy wedge known as the British chip!'

'Why have all the vehicles got 32 on their number plates?' asked Ben.

'That's the number of the *département* and we are in Gers, which is 32. Paris is 75 and the Dordogne 24, those are the only ones I know,' said Kate.

'Fancy you poms owning all this once,' remarked Joey, who had read Kate's book on Gascony with interest.

'Yes, pity we lost it when you think about it,' answered Kate.

'It was Eleanor of Aquitaine's domain,' Ben stated. 'The lands came to the English crown when she married Henry II.'

Joey and Kate both expressed surprise at Ben's knowledge.

'History was the only subject I enjoyed at school, and the only thing I was any good at. I was fascinated by the stories of knights in shining armour and the great Plantagenet kings of England. Their lives seemed so colourful and romantic but of course in reality, they were cruel and unscrupulous by the standards of today and I should imagine pretty dirty as well!'

'When did you lot lose all this then?' asked Joey.

'I think we were finally kicked out in 1453 at the Battle of Castillon – rather a long time ago I'm afraid!'

'That's pretty interesting,' said Joey, 'but to change the subject, why don't we ask the monsieur if he knows of a vineyard we could visit? He must know about local wine producers as most of the stuff on his list is Côtes de Gascogne.'

'Might as well,' agreed Kate. 'You going to ask him?'

'Don't be stupid!' giggled Joey, 'I can't get any further than *bonjour* and *comment allez-vous!*'

Kate raised a questioning eyebrow at Ben.

'Count me out - I can only just do the *bonjour* bit!'

'Well, let's hope he understands my amazing French.'

The swarthy little Gascon waitress arrived at that moment with three cups of strong black coffee and an Armagnac for Ben. Having learnt that the brandy was the pride of the region, he decided the time had come to try some.

Ben had been watching a man at the next door table out of the corner of his eye, and had noticed the way he twirled the balloon glass, inhaling deeply of the amber liquid's aroma before taking a sip and swallowing appreciatively. He wanted to look sophisticated and impress the girls, particularly Joey, with his manly knowledge of brandy drinking. Unfortunately, as he swirled the Armagnac round the glass he was a bit too violent, and some slopped out and fell onto his trousers. Ignoring his error, he sunk his nose into the balloon and inhaled deeply. The fumes shot up his nose like a fireball and brought tears to his eyes. He swallowed a mouthful, and coughing and spluttering, realised that all his assumed savoir-faire was lost as Joey and Kate burst out laughing.

'Oh Ben!' Kate laughed, 'that was the best thing I've seen in years – you are divine! Come on, give us a swig,' and she took the glass and tried the Armagnac. 'Hmm, it *is* a pretty rough one, rather fiery and lacking quality I should say.'

Joey put her hand on Ben's arm and gave it a reassuring squeeze. 'Don't worry,' she said, 'I've never tasted the stuff either and I'm not sure I want to, judging by your face!'

But Ben had seen the funny side of his efforts to appear sophisticated and passed the glass to Joey. 'Go on, just have a sip and see what you think.'

Joey obliged but wrinkled up her nose in distaste.

'*Urgh*! No thanks, it's far too strong for me - I think I'll stick to wine.'

'Not all Armagnacs taste like that,' said Kate. 'My father has some at home that tastes much smoother and doesn't blow your head off when you sniff it.'

'I *would* like to learn about it,' said Ben, 'will you ask the *patron* or whatever you call him, Kate? He's sure to know where we could visit.'

'Your wish is my command, sire!' answered Kate, surprised at Ben's unusual flash of authority.

Le Patron was standing in the doorway, surveying his contented customers, when Kate caught his eye and beckoned him over to their table.

'*Monsieur, s'il vous plaît, nous désirons visiter un château pour apprendre un peu de la production du vin et de l'Armagnac. Est-il possible connaissez-vous?*'

Kate's schoolgirl French appeared to be adequate, for

the Frenchman nodded and smiled and disappeared inside, reappearing a minute later with a small brochure.

'*Voila!*' he declared proudly, handing the paper to Kate with a flourish. '*Je connais bien Monsieur Dubuc, le propriétaire. Il est un homme très bien informé, très gentil et son contremaître parle L'Anglais.*'

'*Merci beaucoup Monsieur,*' answered Kate. '*Peut-être nous allons lui chercher demain.*'

'*Je vous en prie.*' He gave a little bow and hurried off.

'Well *mes amis*, it seems we're in luck. Not only a polite, switched-on owner, but a foreman who speaks English.'

'That's just as well,' commented Ben. 'The visit would have been pretty useless if we couldn't understand anything. I shall look forward to that.' He finished his Armagnac with one swig and sat back in his chair. 'And now, if you ladies are ready, I would like to go back and have a swim.'

The idea appealed to the girls, and having paid the bill and bid their fellow diners *bonsoir*, Ben drove them home through the halcyon Gascon night.

After breakfast the following morning, Kate telephoned Monsieur Dubuc, to find out when it might be convenient for them to arrive for a conducted tour of his vineyard. She explained how they had acquired his name, and how helpful it would be if his English speaking *contremaître* could show them round.

M. Dubuc was, as the restaurateur had said, charming and helpful. If they liked to arrive at 5 o'clock, Stefan would be free to show them round and after, he himself would be delighted to join them for a little *dégustation* of his products.

Kate put the phone down and went outside to tell the other two the good news. 'It's all on for this afternoon, 5 o'clock. I reckon it should take us about 15 minutes, so let's leave just after 4.30 to allow for getting lost.'

'I'll have a look at the map before we go,' suggested Ben, 'and then with any luck, we might not get lost!'

Thanks to Ben's navigation, they drew up in front of the château at two minutes past five. Joey expressed disappointment at the modesty of the house that called itself a château. But as Kate pointed out, the châteaux of Gascony were seldom the grandiose buildings of the Loire.

'I think it's lovely,' said Ben, 'and, what's more, you could easily imagine living in it. Those other places we saw on the way down were unreal.'

The château sat serene and confident, unchanged since it was built towards the end of the 17th century. The afternoon sun shone golden on the yellow-grey stone, the faded burgundy red shutters still closed against its heat. Four squat, round towers stood at each corner and the russet tiles on the gently pitched roof capped them neatly, finishing with a blunt point at the apex.

A dusty old mongrel dog sat scratching itself on the gravel outside what appeared to be the front door, but otherwise there was no sign of life.

'What shall we do now?' wondered Joey.

'Get out and find somebody,' replied Kate. 'They know we're coming. Come on Ben, you're the man, you lead the way.'

But as they got out of the car, a scrunch of feet on gravel proclaimed life, and a tall blond man in his thirties came round the corner.

'You are Miss Amberly and friends I presume. Welcome to Château Lescoubet, I am Stefan Joubert.'

His English was fluent, yet there was a hint of an accent which Kate found difficult to identify, though she was certain it was not French.

Stefan Joubert was wearing jeans and a polo shirt, and was one of the best looking men Kate had ever seen. And he had the body and manner to go with it.

'How do you do.' Kate shook hands and introduced her friends. 'Please call me Kate, Miss Amberly makes me sound like a school mistress!'

His handshake was firm and dry and the hairs on his strong forearms were bleached pale on his tanned skin.

'Wow!' mouthed Kate at Joey, eyebrows raised as she turned away after the introductions. Joey grinned and pinched her friend. 'He's got a wedding ring on,' she whispered quickly as Stefan and Ben began to walk on towards a field of vines.

'Just my luck!'

As the two girls caught up, Stefan began to tell them about the work of the château.

'The wine we make here is all white and is our biggest production. This is quite a new venture, only perhaps 25 years but it is good for commerce. However, our pride and joy is the Armagnac. The family of Monsieur Dubuc has been making fine Armagnac at Lescoubet for nearly three hundred years.'

'Gosh!' exclaimed Joey, impressed. 'That's incredible.'

'Yes,' smiled Stefan, 'I think he knows a little bit about it! Now see these vines here, they are called *folle blanche*. It is they and the *ugni blanc* that are grown for the Armagnac.'

'Can you tell the difference?' asked Ben, gazing at the acres of vines stretching away into the distance. 'They all look the same to me.'

'Oh yes, when you know them and work with them it is easy to learn to identify the different varieties. I would be a poor oenologist if I could not do so.'

'What's a oenologist?' asked Joey.

'A wine-maker. The word comes from the Greek *oinos* meaning wine, and it takes much study and I think a little instinct, to be a good one. The blending and treatment of the wine is very important for reliable quality, but Monsieur Dubuc is the wizard when it comes to the

Armagnac. He is a Gascon and he has the feel in his blood, he comes from this soil.'

'There must be some work goes into looking after all these vines,' commented Kate, 'I had no idea there would be so many and all trained on wires and beautifully kept.'

'A great deal of the work is done mechanically these days, even harvesting, but we still need many people to help. Now in June, the vines must be sprayed with sulphur – the funny odour you can smell – now we hope for good weather for the flowers that will be grapes.

After the three had inspected the vines and Stefan had talked some more about their care, he led them back towards the buildings.

'I am sorry that you have not come at a time when there is much to see working, but if you like I can explain what will happen when the *vendange*, that is the harvest, begins.'

'Yes please, if you have time,' said Ben, who seemed fascinated by the whole process.

'But of course. We will begin with a look at the *vendangeuse*, the machine that picks the grapes.' They set off to inspect the sleeping giant which would roar into life in the autumn and smash the juicy grapes from the vines. Stefan showed them the pit where the grapes were tipped to begin their journey into wine, and the press which squashed them.

'No men and women dancing barefoot in old wooden tubs,' remarked Kate wistfully.

The succession of augers and pipes which carried the residue here and the juice there; filters, fomenters, great stainless steel vats, and more temperature gauges and concrete than the three open mouthed listeners had ever imagined.

'Goodness!' said Ben, his head reeling with information, 'I had no idea that wine making was such a mechanised process. All this equipment makes my milking machines look like chicken feed.'

Stefan shrugged. 'Why do it by hand when you can do it by machine. I don't suppose your milk tastes any different now than when the milkmaid sat under the cow.'

'I know what Ben means though,' said Joey, 'I kind of imagined something much more traditional and rustic, though I suppose I had never really thought much about it.'

'Now we shall look at something a little more rustic, as you put it, so please follow me.'

Stefan led the way to another building where he opened a door at the end of a short passage. Inside stood a great copper creature, all pipes, cauldrons and coils, and looking for all the world like something out of a wizard's kitchen.

'What on earth is that?' cried Kate as they gazed at it in amazement.

'*That*,' announced Stefan proudly, 'is Monsieur Dubuc's *alembic*. It is the still which turns the wine into spirit, and in this extraordinary contraption lies the secret of his Armagnac. Of course there are many other factors which contribute to the character of the brandy; the soil, the grapes, the weather and the length of time the spirit remains in the casks. But it is when this beautiful creature is alive' - he stroked the copper affectionately as he spoke - 'that Monsieur Dubuc comes alive also, for he is the master.'

'Oh!' breathed Ben, entranced, 'I would love to see it working.'

'Unfortunately that is only possible if you come in December when it burns night and day until all is finished. Monsieur Dubuc is very particular about the wood that is used to fire the *alembic*, and he seldom leaves its side once the process has begun. But now we must move on to the *chai*. I think your desire for the rustic will like this, Joey.'

Joey did. An incredible complexity of massive oak timbers formed the ancient roof of the *chai*, which was dark and cool, the air redolent of that which it guarded.

Vast wooden vats lined one wall, and piled upon each other in rows were dozens of dark oak barrels. They sat silent and dusty, while their precious contents matured to create the liquid pride of Gascony.

'We must go now,' said Stefan, looking at his watch. 'Monsieur Dubuc wishes to meet you and sample with you some of his products.'

'There is so much more I'd like to know,' said Ben as they left the *chai*.

'It would take me many, many hours to explain it all,' replied Stefan. 'The entire subject is most complex and full of variety. Maybe you would like to come again, but I think perhaps the ladies have seen enough.' His serious face creased into a rare smile as he looked at Ben.

'I'd love to, but I don't want to be a nuisance. You must be very busy.'

'It would be no nuisance for me, provided you can come at the same time when most of my work is finished for the day. Let us say the day after tomorrow?'

'Fine, and thanks – I'll be here.'

Monsieur Dubuc and the dusty dog awaited them in the doorway of one of the round towers. *'Bonjour, mesdemoiselles et monsieur, entrez s'il vous plaît.'*

He was short and strong with a nut-brown face. On his head he wore a black Gascon beret and his smile was as warm and frequent as Stefan's was rare.

'Asseyez, asseyez,' he smiled, waving a stubby arm towards the chairs placed by a round wooden table that fitted the tower perfectly. The walls were washed white and there was nothing else in the room.

Kate wished her French was better, for she could understand little of what the Gascon said. He talked like a machine gun, his accent all *ang* and *ac*, and she was soon lost.

Endless bottles were produced, each one more extolled than the last, and they sniffed, swirled and tasted for nearly an hour. It was with reeling heads that they finally arose to leave; Kate determined to try a short speech of thanks in French.

'*Merci beaucoup Monsieur pour votre gentillesse. Mes amis et moi avons pris beaucoup de plaisir lors de notre visite à votre château. Je suis triste qu'il est impossible pour vous et moi parlé.*'

Monsieur Dubuc roared with kindly laughter at Kate's French, and taking her hand in his work-worn fingers, kissed it. '*Enchanté, Mademoiselle, enchanté,*' and he rushed off, returning a few seconds later with three little sample bottles of Armagnac which he presented to each one of the three friends in turn. Many *merci-s* later, they shuffled out to the car and Ben drove slowly back to Le Rouchinon.

*

'Don't forget I've arranged to go to Lescoubet again today,' said Ben, when two days later they were making their plans for the day over breakfast.

'I think if you don't mind Ben, I'll give it a miss,' said Joey. 'I'm not sure my head can stand any more Armagnac – physical or mental.'

'Kate?'

'Sorry Ben, the lure of the pool is even greater than the gorgeous Stefan!'

'Would it be OK if I took the car then?'

'Of course it would,' answered Kate, 'and we'll have a magnificent barbecue waiting upon your return.'

'We'd better get going,' said Joey, 'it's market day today and we'll miss all the best shellfish if we're late. Let's get some mussels and have *moules marinière* as a starter.'

'Sounds fine to me, I really feel like a good blow out tonight! You going to shave Ben, or are we into designer stubble?'

'Give me five minutes and I'll be in the car. You two can do the shopping while I go and inspect the cattle market. I want to have a good look at these Blonde d'Aquitaine beasts the Frogs are so keen on.'

'Ben's very taken up with it all, isn't he?' said Joey, after Ben had gone off to shave. 'I've been really surprised by how much he's come out of his shell since we left England.'

'Still waters run deep!' replied Kate, 'but yes, I agree with you – if only Stefan was as interested in me as he is in Ben, I could leave you two to get on with it and go frolicking in the vines with our luscious guide!'

'I told you, you idiot, he's got a wedding ring.'

'My dear innocent little sheila, since when was fidelity assured by a band of gold! But he gives off no vibes worst luck, and although I'm not exactly rampant, a bit of lust wouldn't go amiss.'

'D'you miss Henry?'

'Not one bit - he was about as boring in bed as he was out of it. That's the trouble really, as soon as the novelty of sex with a new man wears off, the whole thing becomes drab. I just can't imagine what it must be like to live with the same man for evermore, like my parents for example. Snoring, nagging, ageing bodies – I bet they never do *it*!'

'Honestly Kate, you do have a cynical view of marriage and men. There is such a thing as love and companionship that can exist without lust you know.'

'I think you rather fancy Ben on the quiet! Seriously though, I'm really glad he came even though we haven't had a puncture yet for him to mend. He's been great company and I think he's really enjoyed himself so far.'

'I hope so,' said Joey with feeling. 'Look, we'd better make a shopping list, there are loads of things like butter and olive oil that we need, as well as all the food for tonight.'

'You make the list and I'll start the dishwasher – here's Ben, all shaven and fragrant so we had better hurry up.'

The market was humming, and pit-stops at the numerous cafes impossible to resist. By the time the trio returned to Le Rouchinon, they were hot and tired and Ben only had half an hour before leaving for his rendezvous with Stefan at Château Lescoubet.

'Have fun and see you later,' said Joey as he left them beside the pool. Kate was deep in her book.

'Sorry to disturb you, but could you put some oil on my back?' asked Joey.

'Shall I tell you something, Joanne Channon,' said Kate, squirting oil on her friend's brown back, 'I definitely do think you are rather keener on that man than you would have me believe. There's something about the way you two look at each other that wasn't there before.'

'Oh not that old thing again, you were on about it this morning!'

'Well, am I right or not?'

'Aah!' Joey sighed, 'well yes, you could be! I have grown rather fond of him.'

'Being *fond's* no good, that's for old age if you're lucky. The point is, do you lust after his body, and do you ache to have him slip between your juicy thighs for a night of frenzied, sweaty passion!'

'Really Kate!' Joey laughed, 'I think he would run a mile.'

'Don't you be so sure. He's a lot more self-assured than when I first met him and the old testosterone should be coursing through his veins at his age.'

'I must admit, I wouldn't say *no*, but he seems more interested in cows and Armagnac than me.'

'Give him the eye, waggle your comely body about a bit and see what happens. Sex is for now, not the distant future, you know. It's a pleasurable experience like eating *foie gras* or tasting a fine wine, so you might as well get on and have it while you can.'

'I shall take your advice to heart and see what I can do!' laughed Joey, floating away into the middle of the pool on her lilo.

Ben returned late, full of enthusiasm and new knowledge. Sausages and chops were sizzling on the barbecue and they were soon sitting round the table on the terrace, consuming *moules marinière* and wine.

'I hope you two don't mind, but I've asked Stefan to come to supper tomorrow,' said Ben.

'Of course not,' replied Joey. 'Good idea, he's been very kind about showing us Lescoubet.'

'What about his wife?' asked Kate.

'She's away in Paris apparently. Actually he seemed rather vague about her.'

'Even better!' joked Kate, 'I might get a look in.'

'There's something a bit odd about him you know,' Ben continued thoughtfully.

'Like what?' Joey questioned.

'I don't know, that's the silly thing, I can't put my finger on it. But he's been very kind as you say, and he jumped at my casual invitation, almost too eagerly.'

'Perhaps he hasn't been here very long or made many friends. He's not French, I'm sure of that,' remarked Kate.

'Oh well, no doubt we shall find out more tomorrow. He's probably just fed up with having to fend for himself while his wife's away. Bread please Joey – I could eat this bread for ever!'

Stefan arrived the next evening on the dot of 7.30. Kate had only just finished her evening swim and was busy changing, for once making an effort with her appearance. She watched him from her bedroom window as he got out of the car and walked across the courtyard towards the front door. His pale, stone-coloured chinos were spotless and he wore a dark green Lacoste polo shirt. Everything about him looked stylish and immaculate and his highly polished brown shoes were decorated with little leather tassels.

Englishmen never look quite like that, thought Kate, quickly putting on a clean T-shirt and dash of lip gloss.

The other three were already seated with their drinks when Kate joined them a few minutes later, and Stefan rose to his feet to greet her.

'Good evening, Kate. It is most kind of you all to invite me to join you.'

'Not at all, we've taken up a lot of your time and it's been very interesting for us to look round Lescoubet. We wouldn't have got very far without an English speaking guide!'

'How come you speak such good English?' asked Joey.

'Ah well, you see I spent some time studying in England after leaving school because I knew it would help me to get a good job. We do a lot of business with the UK and the States, so English is a very important language for us – you are fortunate that you did not have to learn to speak it!'

There was a slight pause in the conversation while Joey went to fetch some more nuts and Ben refilled the glasses.

'Stefan's bought two bottles of Château Lescoubet wine for us to try,' said Ben.

'That's kind, I shall look forward to drinking it,' said Kate. 'I'm sure it will be better than our house plonk we get from the supermarket – no need to swirl or sniff this stuff, just swallow it!'

Stefan permitted himself a slight smile at Kate's remark, and Joey trod on her foot under the table.

'We are sorry your wife couldn't come,' she said, 'it would have been nice to meet her. Ben said she's in Paris.'

There was a slight hesitation before Stefan replied. 'Actually, my wife and I are separated. It is true she is in

Paris, but she lives there now.'

'Oh dear, I'm sorry,' said Joey, I didn't mean to pry.'

'No, no, please do not worry. It is not so unusual that marriages do not work out, and we have no children so our problem was not complicated. We are both happier now the way we are.'

'Have you always lived around here?' asked Ben, anxious to change the subject.

'No,' and again Stefan hesitated, 'I am from Germany originally, I was born in Mannheim.'

'Aha!' Kate butted in, 'that explains your accent. I didn't think it was French, but then your French is so brilliant I couldn't quite make it out. But surely Joubert is a French name, not German?'

'You are quite right about my name, but Joubert is the name of my step-father. My mother and I left Germany when I was a baby, and came to live in France. My father had left us – I never knew him - and in time she married again.'

'It must have been strange for you to change your name like that,' said Ben.

'I was too young to know, and my mother felt it would be easier for me to have a French name. There was still some anti-German feeling in the south-west because of the war.'

'All that old rot!' laughed Kate. 'We shall never get on if we keep harking back to what happened so long ago.'

'I am glad you feel that way, but people have long memories when their country has been invaded.' Stefan paused for a drink before continuing to talk about himself. 'I had an English grandmother you know, so there are genes from both sides in my blood.'

'Oh really,' said Kate sounding interested, 'what part of England did she come from?'

'I know very little about her I am afraid, for she was not much spoken of in the family.'

'Sounds exciting,' said Joey. 'Did she do something awful?'

'She ran away, back to England. She was my father's mother and apparently he never forgave her for leaving him. All I know is that she came from the county of Wiltshire.'

'So you don't know if you've got any cousins lurking around in England?' asked Joey.

'No, I am afraid not.'

'D'you see your mother and step-father much – do they live round here?' asked Kate.

'Sadly my mother died last year, and my step-father moved back to Paris where he came from originally. We make contact from time to time though.'

'Any chance of stopping the inquisition and getting some food?' cut in Ben, who felt Stefan had probably had enough of the girls questioning. 'I don't know about anyone else, but I'm hungry.'

The evening was a success and they even managed to make Stefan laugh when teaching him to play *Old Maid*, which Kate insisted they should do after dinner. They had all drunk just a little too much, but not enough for anything but merriment, and as the moths fluttered round the terrace floodlight, the air became heavy and warm.

'The weather will break soon,' predicted Stefan. 'You see that?' and he pointed to a distant flash. 'That is lightning over the mountains. A heavy storm will be bad for the flowers on the vines but there is nothing we can do. The power of the elements is always greater than the power of man. We are so clever, but finally one greater than us will always win.'

'Well, I hope you're wrong,' said Joey. 'We leave in three days and I don't want it to rain till the last day when we have to clear up the house.'

Stefan seemed dismayed by this news, and turned to Ben. 'But I am sorry to hear this, I thought you would stay for another week. Maybe I shall take you to lunch on this clearing up day. I am sure the ladies are much better at this job than you. We shall try some real Armagnac, some *millésimes* of a great age.'

'Ooh! I say – you chauvinist *cochon*!' cried Kate. 'What do you think, fellow down-trodden female, shall we let them go?'

Joey went and stood behind Ben's chair, chanting 'Eeny meeny miney mo, catch a Pommy by his toe If he hollers let him go, eeny meeny miny mo!'

And she grabbed his nose and twisted it round – 'can't reach your toe!'

'Ouch!' yelled Ben

'Off he goes!' shouted both girls in unison and they all burst out laughing except Stefan, who was unable to understand their English humour.

Ben grabbed Joey's wrist as she went to move away. 'Are you sure you don't mind?' he asked, looking at her brown, smiling face.

'Of course not, do we Kate? You go off for a last fling while we do all the work. You'll only get under our feet anyway!'

He held her arm for a second longer than was necessary and smiled back his thanks.

'It is time for me to leave you,' said Stefan getting to his feet. 'You have given me a wonderful evening and I thank you for your kindness. I shall collect you, Ben, on Friday at noon.'

And they waved him good bye as he drove away down the drive.

The weather hung on for one more day, and as time ran out for the three friends, they crammed as much as they could into the remaining hours of their holiday.

'Why is it that when one's really enjoying life, the time goes so fast?' complained Joey. 'I just can't believe it's Friday and tomorrow we must start back to England.'

'I know,' moaned Kate, 'back to dreary old London and work. Bet my mother rings up tonight to check we haven't burnt the house down. God how boring – reality waits around the corner.'

Ben came into the kitchen to join the other two for coffee and croissant, which he had bought fresh from the local *boulangerie* earlier in the morning.

'I can't believe this is our second last breakfast,' he said, sitting down beside Joey. 'I don't really want to go out to lunch with Stefan you know, I would rather we were all together on our last day.'

'Well, you've got to go, you accepted,' said Kate bossily.

'And we want you out of our hair for the *clearing up day* as your friend calls it,' added Joey. 'And pass the coffee.'

'He's a bit of an odd-ball that Stefan, don't you think?' continued Kate.

'You've said that before,' replied Joey, 'but what you really mean is that the poor fellow is impervious to your charms and has asked Ben to lunch, not you!'

'Hmm, there is that, but joking apart, he's the sort of person who you never know what they're really thinking, d'you know what I mean? Almost creepy in a way.'

'It's probably his German blood,' said Joey, heaping jam on her croissant.

'Maybe,' mused Kate, lighting a cigarette. 'Funny that business about his grandmother coming from Wiltshire though, because my parents had some friends called Goodman who lived in a village there, and I vaguely remember some gruesome story about a woman who was murdered. It was ages ago but the Goodmans came to stay soon after, and kept banging on about it. I was banished from the room but I eaves-dropped.'

'What on earth's that got to do with Stefan or his grandmother?' asked Ben. 'Wiltshire's a big place you know.'

'Nothing I should think, but apparently Mrs. Goodman found the body for some reason, so they became very taken up with the case. The woman had been raped and strangled and the police thought it was a B&B'er who was a German.'

'Did they ever catch him?' asked Joey.

'Not as far as I know but I really haven't a clue. As I said, it was years ago.'

'Honestly Kate,' said Ben, 'poor old Stefan is just an ordinary bloke who happens to be a German with divorced parents and an English grandmother, along with probably several million others.'

'I suppose so,' shrugged Kate, stubbing out her cigarette and getting up. 'I'm going to start sorting the junk in my room. I think it can all go home dirty, I don't like the look of the weather for washing.'

The sky had darkened and the leaves on the tree outside the kitchen window were beginning to rustle as the first breath of the coming wind moved them in its path.

'Me too,' said Joey sadly, 'my room looks as if a tornado's struck!'

'I'll clean out the barbecue and tidy up outside,' volunteered Ben. 'It won't take me five minutes to pack and do my room this evening.'

'Come on then folks, let's get on with it,' said Kate. 'Joey and I want to go shopping later for some things to take home. Is there anything you'd like us to get for you Ben?'

'I don't think so, thanks. I bought some small presents for my family the other day. How do you two feel about going to the restaurant in the square for our last supper?'

As he had anticipated, Ben's suggestion met with approval, for the restaurant he mentioned was a favourite with them all.

Stefan arrived just after noon to take Ben away for their gastronomic lunch, and as Joey went back into the house after waving him away, the telephone rang.

It was Audrey Amberly, and as Kate had predicted, she was checking up on the condition of the house. Joey was able to reassure her that all was well before shouting to Kate to come to the phone.

'Everything OK?' asked Joey, when Kate reappeared a while later, 'you were ages.'

'Yes, fine thanks. Mother wittered on a bit but I think talking to you first did the trick! I got my father on the line though – he's got a memory like an elephant – to ask about the Goodmans and the murdered woman.'

'Really Kate, why are you so obsessed with it, it's not like you and there cannot possibly be any connection.'

'How can you be so sure? Apparently the police were sure it was this German bloke, but he disappeared and they never caught him. But guess what, they found out he lived in Mannheim and his name was Gunther Fernau.'

'So what? Mannheim's a big place and why should Fernau be anything to do with Stefan?'

'Who knows, after all we don't know Stefan's real name.'

'Didn't your father think it odd you asking all these questions?'

'I think he did a bit, but I made up some drivel about a game we played where we each had to tell a true horror story, and when he started his *Really Katherine* bit, I shouted *The line's gone crackly* and put the phone down!'

'Oh Kate!' laughed Joey, 'your poor parents. Anyway, the whole thing's crazy but even if by a million to one chance you're right, and it was Stefan's father, he probably doesn't know anything about it. He would hardly have been born at the time I should think.'

'I expect you're right Joey, and we will never know anyway. Just think though, if his father was a psychopath, chances are he could be a nutter too.'

'Kate, I wish you wouldn't say things like that. I hope Ben will be all right.'

'Don't be daft, of course he will. The best thing for Ben would be for you to get him into your bed! Come on, we had better get on with the shopping before Ben comes rolling home drunk after all Stefan's famous *millésimes*.'

The rain began to fall in great big drops as Joey and Kate drove back from their shopping trip. The dried bodies of numerous insects were stuck to the windscreen, rendering the wipers useless as they smeared a concoction of little legs and blood all over the glass.

'I must clean the windscreen before we leave,' said Kate, peering through the smears.

'Get Ben to do it,' suggested Joey, 'he likes that sort of job.'

'I wonder if he's back yet. Stefan said he was having the afternoon off, I think, so they'll probably be ages.'

'Doesn't matter, we can finish the house, and Ben can load the car in the morning.'

They carried all the shopping into the house and dumped it down on the kitchen table. The thunder rolled nearer and a flash of fork lightning made Joey squeak. 'I hate storms,' she said, 'I know it's silly but they frighten me.'

'Come on, you Aussie drip, we shall batten down the hatches and keep you safe. I thought you lot were supposed to be all tough and open-airish!'

'Thanks cobber. I don't want to let the side down but I have to admit to a certain...'

At that moment, Ben walked in through the kitchen door. He looked strange, and his usual cheerful greeting was absent.

'Hello Ben,' said Joey in surprise,' you're back early. Did you have a good time?'

Ben sat slowly down at the table and ran his hand

through his hair before speaking. 'No Joey,' he said slowly, 'it was awful. I mean the lunch was fantastic, but it was what happened afterwards.'

'Why, whatever happened?' asked Joey, sitting down beside him.

'Tell all,' said Kate eagerly, abandoning her parcels and joining the other two.

'Well, like I said, the lunch was brilliant and I drank an Armagnac that was nearly 100 years old - can you imagine? Then Stefan asked me if I would like to go back to his place for coffee. I said *yes* as it was still quite early, and it seemed a nice idea. I suppose I am rather naïve but well, to cut a long story short, he's gay. I have never been so embarrassed in my life. I felt so sorry for him but had no idea what to say.'

'Oh Ben, poor old you,' Joey took his arm.

'What happened next?' asked Kate, fascinated.

'First he got angry and claimed I'd led him on, of all things, then he started getting all sort of pathetic which was even worse. Then he broke down, and poured out this story his mother told him about how his father had brow-beaten her, and then one day just disappeared into thin air. That's when they moved to France.'

'I'll bet he was the Wiltshire murderer!' cried Kate, banging the table, 'I wonder what happened to him.'

'Probably went to South America I expect,' said Joey. 'He sounded a bit of a Nazi type to me. Anyway, go on Ben, what did you do then?'

'I calmed him down a bit, said I was terribly sorry about it all and asked him to take me home. He never spoke a word and looked kind of weird, as if he was in a trance. When we got back here, I just said thanks for lunch and got out as fast as I could, I can tell you.'

'Make the poor lad some tea Joey - he's had a bit of a shock.'

'I'll say,' she answered, 'I could do with a cup myself.'

And as the thunder crashed overhead and the lights flickered and died, Ben drank his tea in thoughtful silence.

The storm passed, but the rain persisted and when Kate, Joey and Ben arrived at their favourite restaurant in the square, they were unable to sit outside under the old *bastide* arches.

It was hot and smoky inside, but the owner was delighted to see them and the little room buzzed with cheerful French voices.

'I'm going to have the *menu gastronomique*,' announced Kate. 'It's our last night and I'm going for broke. *Foie gras* followed by *confit de canard* and then *croustade*, then I shall probably explode!'

'Why not?' agreed Joey, 'who cares about money or fat when we might all be squashed by a giant *camion* on the way back tomorrow!'

'Hear, hear!' said Ben, determined not to let his earlier experience dampen their last evening, 'and, I'd like to try a decent wine instead of the old *pichet*.'

'Hurry up and order it so we can get stuck in,' said Kate.

'*Monsieur*,' Ben caught the waiter's eye, '*carte du vin s'il vous plaît*.'

'I say Joey,' said Kate, winking at her friend, 'this man has become very dominant all of a sudden!'

'I'd like to try a decent *Madiran* as it comes from not far away,' said Ben when the wine list arrived. He fell to studying it, ignoring Kate's remark. His choice made, he ordered the wine, which arrived a few minutes later.

'*Bien choisi, Monsieur,*' smiled *Le Patron*, as he poured a little for Ben to taste. The girls giggled as he went through the tasting rigmarole and pronounced the wine satisfactory.

'I don't know what you two find so funny,' he said crossly.

'It's nothing Ben,'said Joey, her tone warm and happy. 'It's just that you've changed so much since I first met you on the steps of Flat 11 – and all for the better, I may add.'

Ben took her hand and gave it a small squeeze of thanks.

'Bien choisi indeed, Monsieur Cardew,*'* said Kate, raising her glass to him and drinking deeply.

'Well I think this is an appropriate moment to raise our glasses to you, Kate. This has been the best holiday I've ever had and I can't thank you enough for making it possible.'

'Me too!' joined in Joey, 'I agree with everything Ben said.'

'It's been my pleasure,' replied Kate, 'and I can't think of anyone else I would rather have been with.'

The evening passed, and course after course of delicious food arrived in front of the diners. Bottles littered the table and as the locals drifted away and the old church bell *donged* out eleven, they ordered a last coffee and prepared to leave.

By tacit agreement, there had been no mention of Stefan.

When they arrived back at the house, Kate went straight to bed, claiming that she was tired. Her sixth sense told her that Joey and Ben were on track for a shared bed at last, and she hoped that she was right. She liked the idea of the two of them being in love as they seemed so suited, and in her opinion, some good, honest sex was just what Ben needed.

As Kate lay in bed listening to the rain, she knew her instinct had served her right, for the usual sounds of Joey getting ready for bed in the room next door were absent. *Good for you mate* she thought, before drifting off to sleep.

The following morning dawned overcast and dreary, an ideal day for ending a holiday. Kate was up and about early and, nursing a hangover, had already polished off two large mugs of black coffee by the time the other two appeared in the kitchen. They both looked sheepish and silly in their new-found happiness, and Joey gave Kate a stealthy thumbs-up sign as she sat down.

A scrunch of tyres on the gravel announced the arrival of a car, and they all looked up in surprise.

'Who on earth can that be?' said Joey. 'D'you think it's the owners come to check us out?'

'Not at this hour I shouldn't think, we're not due out till ten,' said Kate, going to look.

'It's the police,' she said. 'What can they want I wonder?' They looked at each other in questioning silence.

A plain clothed man got out of the back of the car and made his way towards the door, leaving the uniformed driver to wait outside. A big bear-like man, he looked rumpled and tired and there were pouchy, grey bags under his eyes. His step was heavy and slow, and Kate had opened the door before he reached the threshold.

'Good morning Mam'selle,' he said in heavily accented English. 'I am Inspector Lefevre. I believe this is where I find Mr. *Carrdu*?'

'Yes, Ben Cardew is here, if that's who you mean,' said Kate rather rudely. Regretting her tone immediately, she apologised. 'I'm sorry, please come in. I'm afraid we don't speak much French.'

The policeman shrugged, and Ben got up from the table as he came into the room. 'I'm Ben Cardew, what's this about?' he asked, his face tight with anxiety. 'Is it to do with my family?'

'Please, sit down - and if I may?'

Ben waved his hand to a chair, wishing he would get on with whatever he had come to say. Policemen seldom brought good news.

'It is not about your family I come Monsieur, it is about

Stefan Joubert. I think you are the friend of this man, yes?'

'I wouldn't say a friend exactly, but I do know him. We all met at Monsieur Dubuc's château earlier in the week when we went to look round the vines.'

'And you see him yesterday?' asked the Frenchman.

'Yes, we had lunch together in Auch.'

'And that is all you do?'

'Well, we went back to his place for coffee and then he drove me home.'

'And was Monsieur Joubert content with your time together?'

'There was a slight misunderstanding between us, but I can assure you, that was all, and as I said, he drove me back here and that's the last time I saw him. Would you mind telling me what this is all about?'

The Inspector sighed wearily, and pulled a crumpled packet of *Gauloise* out of his pocket. Without asking permission he lit one up and, inhaling deeply, leant back in his chair.

'I have to tell you that this morning, Monsieur Dubuc found Stefan Fernau hanging dead in his beautiful Armagnac *chai*. I am sad to say he had disarranged some casks of the precious *Folle Blanche '72*.'

There was a stunned silence round the table, but suddenly Kate spoke out.

'Did you say Stefan Fernau?' she asked urgently, 'why did you call him that?'

'Aah Mam'selle,' he said heavily, 'pardon me but I have the fatigue and my words miss, but that was his name. He take the name Joubert for his mother.'

Kate whistled with astonishment and the other two gasped as they stared at each other in horror.

'Oh no!' cried Ben, breaking the silence. '*How terrible* – poor poor Stefan. Whatever he was, he didn't deserve that – it was not his fault.'

'No,' said Joey slowly, 'it's horrible, we're all very shocked. But why are you asking Ben all these questions Monsieur? He was here with us all the time after he got back from lunch.'

'Because Mam'selle, for us we need the information, but do not have anxiety, there is not what you say *foul play*,' and he allowed himself a wry smile, dropping ash down the front of his rain coat. 'There was a letter he left, but we must make investigation before we shut the book,' and he sighed again, shrugging his broad shoulders. *'Quel dommage!* He was a troubled man with a big weight on him. We are not so foolish as your *Inspector Clouseau* films would have us to be, and we know of his life of difficulty. But now poor Monsieur Dubuc must seek for a new oenologist, and I, Monsieur *Carrdu*, must hear the *gritty-nitty* as you say, of your story.'

'But what did the letter say?' demanded Ben anxiously.

'It say that before she die, his mother tell him *la verite* ....er....how do you say....*trut* about his father and what happen in England. Everything terrible come together and he could not go on.'

Ben's face fell into his hands, and he could find no words.

Kate stood up and turning to Joey, suggested they should leave Ben alone to make his statement to the Inspector.

'It might be easier for him if the Inspector wants all the lurid details of Stefan's leap – you know, man to man and all that!' she said when they were alone in Kate's bedroom.

'The whole thing is absolutely incredible,' said Joey, shaking her head. 'I never believed in a million years that your crazy theory about Stefan's father and that woman could be right. No wonder the poor guy was in a mess.'

'I entirely blame his father - people like that shouldn't be allowed to breed,' said Kate. 'After all, if Stefan had

had a normal father, I'm dead sure he would have been a normal, happy man.'

'I agree,' replied Joey vehemently. 'Rotten luck on the poor kid when it's got no choice, and what's such a big deal about fancying your own sex anyway – there's nothing wrong with it.'

To their relief, it was not long before they heard the front door shut and sounds of the police car driving away. Joey hurried through to find Ben, who was still sitting in the kitchen staring at the wall, chin resting in the palms of his hands. She put her arms around him and held him tight.

'Thank goodness that's all over,' she said, kissing the top of his head.

'Oh Joey,' he sighed sadly, 'I feel awful about it, as if I'd killed him almost.'

'That's nonsense Ben, and you know it. Like the Inspector said, he was a deeply troubled man, and if he was that unbalanced, then anything could have tipped him over the edge at any time. It was not your fault in any way.'

'No – but maybe if I'd known more about his state of mind, I could have helped in some way. It seems such a waste of a life.'

'I don't know Ben,' replied Joey. 'But I suspect he was in need of more help than you could possibly have given him.'

'Come on you two,' said Kate, desperately trying to lighten the atmosphere while dragging a load of luggage into the kitchen. 'You've got a lifetime ahead for all that lovey-dovey stuff but if we don't get a move on now, we shall miss the ferry tonight.'

'Shall we drink one last toast before we go?' said Joey, 'there's an open bottle somewhere which we'll only have to chuck away.'

'Why not!' said Kate, going to look for the bottle.

'Oh look,' she said, returning a minute later, 'it's Château Lescoubet!'

Ben filled three glasses and threw the bottle in the bin.

'We'll drink two toasts,' he said, 'one to the man who had no chance, and one to those that have.'

'To Stefan,' said Ben, 'may he rest in peace,' and they raised their glasses and stood in silence for a moment.

'And to us, the lucky ones.'

Half an hour later, everything was crammed into the car, and the three friends were ready to leave. Kate took a last look round Le Rouchinon, pausing a moment to fill her memory with all that had been. 'Thank you house,' she said aloud, 'I wonder if we shall ever come back.' But the house remained silent. The holiday was over, and it was time to go back to the real world.

77686249R00116

Made in the USA
Middletown, DE
24 June 2018